A DARKER BREATH

A Ben Weir Mystery

Neil Slade

To Judy

With all best wishes.

Neil Sl

A Darker Breath

© 2019 by Neil Slade

ISBN-13: 978-1723476686

ISBN-10: 1723476684

Cover Design: SelfPubBookCovers.com/3rustedspoons

Chapter 1

Professor David Weir sat back from his monitor and rolled his aching shoulders, groaning as he felt the stiffened muscles object. As usual he hadn't realised how long he'd spent sitting glued to the data sets on the screen in front of him. He had a good feeling about this latest break through; well at least the initial plating tests were looking promising. He stood up and stretched his back out; sitting for long hours was not good for him. He wandered over to the coffee pot and sniffed at the dark brown liquid; a fresh brew or part stewed? He really couldn't be bothered to set up the filter again and went for part stewed, the extra strength might renew his thought processes.

Finally the investment in CordyGen might be on the brink of paying off. It wasn't the money he was worried about but the effect it might have on his career if it failed. His decision to side step away from the purely academic route had his colleagues puzzled at the time, but if he was to really succeed Weir knew he needed the autonomy over his research that setting up his own company would bring. The first few trials of the various extracts from the *Cordyceps* fungus had proved of little value, but completing the DNA sequencing and being able to target specific genes had given their results a huge boost. Since he and his team had published the DNA sequencing papers, interest in their venture had renewed and money had flowed their way from interested investors.

David jumped at the sound of his office phone. He stared at it, his brow creased in puzzlement, who'd be calling him on the office line on a Sunday afternoon, it's not as if it's normal working hours.

He picked up the receiver and after a second's hesitation said 'David Weir, hello?'

'Hello darling. Are you remembering to get up and move about, you know what your back can be like?' Weir smiled at the sound of his wife's voice.

'Yes Helen, in actual fact I was just standing and stretching when you called. What are you doing phoning on the landline?'

'Because I know you. You're mobile is probably buried in the bottom of your briefcase and when you're immersed in writing, the Walls of Jericho could tumble down around your ears and you'd have no idea. I reckoned the landline was the best way to get through to you.' She sounded breathy as if she was walking.

After twenty-three years of marriage there was little that Helen Weir didn't know about how her husband functioned. He might be one of the foremost world authorities on *Ascomycete* fungi and antibiotic development but he would also leave the house with odd socks if she wasn't on the ball.

'Anyway let me in in five minutes will you. I'm just calling for coffee and sandwiches from the deli and I have the typing you wanted for tomorrow. I thought I'd bring it with me now rather than you having to bring it with you tomorrow.'

Weir smiled again. Not only was Helen a perfect wife she was also a perfect personal assistant. Since

5

they had both completed their PhDs her own scientific career had been put in second place to his. Clichéd of course, but in fact without Helen's insights into some of the advancements the combined weight of CordyGen's scientific team wouldn't have got as far as it had. That was one of the reasons he insisted Helen's name was added to the relevant research papers even though she wasn't strictly one of the research and development team.

'Sure thing. I'll ring down and let Benny know you're on your way. Oh and can I have bacon and avocado on brown if they have any?'

'Coming right up.'

After he had alerted Benny, the security guard manning the reception at weekends, David wandered down the corridor to his own laboratory. He pulled out a stack of petri dishes and laid them side-by-side on the bench examining the results of the latest trial with CDY1963. He was in no doubt of the antibiotic usefulness against strains of bacteria resistant to many of the common antibiotics. What this particular trial showed was that they had successfully managed to splice the gene for CDY1963 production into benign bacteria so that they could mass-produce the chemical. They were one step nearer to being able to offer a new and potent antibiotic to the medical world. Once it had passed human trials its application would be widespread; of course there's no doubt that antibiotic resistance would eventually develop, but by then he would have hoped CordyGen to have added more new discoveries to the pharmacopeia.

He turned at the sound of the laboratory door opening and smiled as Helen's head popped round. "Come on, lunch is on the desk.' She disappeared again as David replaced the petri dishes back in the incubator and returned to his office. Kissing Helen he sat down as she handed him his coffee.

'I just wanted to show you this before we eat.' Helen pulled up a chair to David's desk and sat next to him placing a pile of paper clipped papers in front of him. She quickly skipped through the documents until she found the one she wanted. David noticed his own handwritten scrawl on lined paper slipped in between the pristine white sheets of printed paper. It always amazed him that Helen could decipher his jottings and turn them into drafts of papers in preparation for scientific submission or investor reports.

Helen pulled out a sheet of charts and statistical analysis. 'You know how I am about typing up this sort of thing. I'm pretty sure it's all okay, but I'd rather you went over it in particular to check. It's so easy to get something the wrong way round and of course...I'm dealing with your handwriting!'

David laughed and pulled the two pieces of paper together and placed them on one side. 'I'm sure it is all perfect, but I will go through it, later though not now. I've been staring at that computer so long I'm in danger of going bog eyed.' He cleared a space on his desk, 'So where's this sandwich?' While he was deep in work mode David hadn't even thought about food, but since Helen had mentioned it his stomach was in overdrive telling him how hungry he was.

'Ben called this morning. Everything is fine, but he's looking to getting this week out of the way. He's got five more mock exams and then everything is finished. They seem to be testing the boys to death but I assume with GCSEs coming up in the next term they have to keep them on the ball.'

'I should think so too! We're not paying all that money for him to have a whale of a time. As much as he might moan about it a good strong academic grounding is the springboard for success in life…God I sound like my father!'

David's heritage was littered with academics, most of them medical or scientists of various disciplines. He had to admit it was in his blood.

'Well if Ben does half as well as his father he'll be doing okay. But you know him, if he can wing it he will in favour of getting out on that rugby pitch.'

David took a bite of the sandwich and revelled in the squishy feel of the avocado against the crunch of the crispy bacon as the flavours teased over his tongue. His taste ecstasy was suddenly broken by the concern in Helen's voice.

'What's that?'

David looked at his computer screen, which a minute earlier had been showing a page of results data. Now it was blank, a black screen with a red heart at its centre, swelling and decreasing in size. At the same time the room was filled with the soft double sound rhythm of a heart beat. David tapped the return button on the keyboard but it had no effect. He hit the escape button, still no effect. He swore under his breath and tapped it several times; his finger jabbing down harder with each strike.

'Did you save it?' Helen asked tentatively.

'All but the last ten minutes or so, so it's not too much to lose and redo.' David sighed and hit the Ctrl-Alt-Delete buttons to try to reboot the system.

The throbbing heart taunted them like a beacon, it's image reflected in David's glasses as he stared at the screen, his brow furrowed. 'What the…?' The heart was now joined by a message in shimmering dancing letters, *Thank you Professor David Weir. Your research will prove most invaluable, but now I am afraid it is time to say 'Goodbye'.*

'Shut it down!' Helen's voice was as frantic as David now felt. His system had clearly been hacked and it looked like someone had been systematically stealing his research. He dropped his sandwich on the desk, pieces of mayonnaise-covered avocado spilling out onto his research papers, sliding off his chair he was on his hands and knees scrabbling for wires. It was then that he spotted the device taped to the backboard of his desk; it's red flashing light mocking him like the beating heart on his monitor screen. A cold wave of fear ran through his body as his racing mind suddenly realised what he was looking at. He'd just enough time to scream his wife's name before the blast ripped his office apart. At the same time as the bomb under his desk detonated, several others went off reducing the building, and CordyGen, to a blazing inferno.

Chapter 2

Ben could walk to the parish church from Luxborough House in ten minutes, and that was without rushing, but the journey by car following the two hearses that carried his parents' coffins seemed to take forever. He sat stiffly, looking out of the window without registering the familiar sights that he had seen for most of his childhood. Uncle Simon sat on one side of him lost in his own thoughts. It was the first time Ben had seen his father's brother for several months and on the other side, Aunt Evelyn. Where his mother was calm and warm, her sister was anxiety ridden and brittle. Since the news she had been her usual cold self, spending most of her time sniping at her hen pecked husband, but now the funeral was actually happening she had withdrawn into her own thoughts. Sitting purse lipped and upright, her hands clasped together in her lap, she had not taken her eyes off the back of the hearse in front of the funeral car.

As Ben looked forward he couldn't stop random thoughts coming into his head. Was his dad's coffin in the lead or his mum's? He thought of them lay in their wooden boxes as if asleep, arms crossed over their chests like in the films he'd seen. But in reality what was in the coffins. They had been right next to the main bomb and the fire had been intense. There couldn't possibly have been much left of them. Were the coffins empty and just symbolic, if so what was the point or were they full of a pile of ash, pieces of charred flesh? Thankfully, before his thoughts could get more extreme, they had climbed up the hill from Luxborough House and were at the church.

The cars drew up to a crowd waiting at the end of the drive leading up to the west door. Ben scanned their faces, he knew many of them by name, others by sight; friends, work colleagues, academic associates. He was pleased that he was centre stage in a way; it meant that people couldn't really get near him. He didn't want to speak to any of them, hear their sympathies. If he had his way he'd have been off across the North Downs with his thoughts. The family group stood to one side watching while the coffins were placed on collapsible tumbrils and then wheeled respectfully by the bearers up the long sloping drive; large oak trees flanking like sentinels along the way.

Most people were dressed in black; the sight making Ben think of a massing of crows or penguins huddled together in the Antarctic wind. At the tops of the trees a flock of jackdaws were calling loudly to each other, their chorus of calls sounding as if they were chuckling and mocking the events below.

'Here we go Ben,' Simon said quietly. He placed an arm across Ben's shoulders and steered him behind the coffins up the driveway and into the church, the remainder following behind.

When they arrived back at Luxborough House a large buffet had been carefully arranged along the length of the long dining room table. Mrs. Jessop had drafted in some people from the town to help her so that she could get away for the funeral. Mourners filed in and soon most of the bottom floor of the house was full of people standing in groups chatting over sandwiches and glasses of white wine.

Ben had been fending off comments of condolence with a smile and a nod, before turning away from the person cutting off any chance of in depth discussions. He'd had enough of concerned masks and wrinkled brows as they turned to face him. He didn't care if he appeared rude, but at the same time knew that excuses would be made for him anyway, shock and all that. Why couldn't they all just go and leave him alone.

Ben managed to find himself an empty chair tucked away in the corner of one of the sitting rooms. He sat trying to make himself small and invisible, nursing a plate of sandwiches Mrs. Jessop had piled up for him. He hadn't realised until then just how hungry he was and consumed them rapidly. He was weighing up the protocol of going next door to get a second helping when he spied Charles Gleeson coming in. Gleeson looked directly at Ben and started to make his way across, but was deflected by two men who had been deep in conversation and drew Gleeson in before he could get to Ben. Seeing his chance of escape Ben slipped out through the French windows and into the back garden.

Gleeson was the deputy director of his father's company; a fast ascending star in the world of antibiotic development, always in the right place at the right time. Since he'd joined CordyGen as a postdoctoral researcher he had seen off any competition and quickly risen up the company hierarchy. Ben's parents had had many a heated discussion about him, with Helen cautioning David. His father seemed to think that Gleeson was just ambitious and that trait should be encouraged because it was ambition that drove success and success that developed the antibiotics and brought in the funding money.

Ben agreed with his mother. Gleeson was a slime ball who was in it for himself. Whenever he visited he would always make a show of being interested in Ben; what he was doing, was he going to be a scientist like him and his dad, even down to 'there'd be a research place for him at CordyGen'. As if that was really up to him! Then in the next second it was as if Ben had suddenly disappeared into a black hole, the sycophantic 'show interest in the kid' box checked, Gleeson had moved on.

No doubt Gleeson was trying to get to Ben now because with his father's death the position of Director and Chief Executive Officer was vacant. Ben had no idea what would happen with his father's company, and didn't particularly want to know either.

As he walked past one of the windows of his father's study he glanced in. It was empty; a place of sanctuary. Going in through the front door he managed to slip through the wide hall without too much difficulty. He could hear familiar voices deep in conversation. Aunt Evelyn holding court about what would happen to Ben and how she would step into the breach, although of course she '…wouldn't expect to replace his mother'. The whine of Gleeson's high pitched nasal voice, almost sounding like he was still waiting for it to break, discussing something scientific, no doubt with the two men who had blocked his attempt to get to Ben.

He heaved a sigh of relief as he got to the sanctuary of his father's study. The door wasn't locked but someone, probably Mrs. Jessop with her foresight, had blue tacked a sign to the door with '*Private*' in large black letters on it.

Ben opened the door and slipped through closing it quietly behind him. Instantly the hubbub of conversation was transformed to a muted murmur. He looked around the familiar room, his father's kingdom. It was untouched since the last time his father had sat behind the big oak desk. It had that familiar mixed scent of dusty and musty from all the books and papers. Mrs. Jessop had long since given up the task of trying to clean it with the same frequency as the other rooms in the house.

He walked over to his favourite spot, a window half covered by a bookcase which, when installed alongside its neighbour, overhung the wall for about three feet blocking out half the window. He remembered when his father had first installed it, his mother was not amused, but had to defer to the fact it was 'her husband's room' and just as he wanted it. The wide windowsill had been covered with a long cushion making a window seat and as a child Ben would sit there tucked behind the bookcase so nobody inside the room could see him. He would read or watch birds from the window or, if he was very quiet, he could listen to his father work.

He took off his suit jacket and folding it up, tucked it behind his back as he took up his familiar place. He pulled his legs up hugging his knees and thought of his parents, as hot, silent tears ran down his cheeks.

Ben's solitude was short lived. He held his breath as he heard the study door open and two people entered the room.

'This really isn't the time for this conversation Charles.' Uncle Simon said firmly.

'Oh yes, I appreciate the circumstances, who wouldn't, but with needing to finalise the grant from the Wellcome Trust I just need an assurance of where I stand. Then there's the no small task of rebuilding the company after the accident. I'll be having to make decisions that are really above my employment grade.' Gleeson's nasal whine continued on, 'I tried to have a word with Ben earlier but he seems to have disappeared.'

Ben heard his uncle sigh and clear his throat. Gleeson carried on regardless, 'We both know Ben's probably going to be left the company and I expect with you as some sort of guardian. So with backing from you both for me to become the new Director in Chief and company CEO it makes any decisions by the board academic really. You must see that.' Gleeson's voice had got higher and his speech faster no doubt as he could see the growing irritation develop on Simon's face.

'Now listen to me Gleeson,' Simon snapped, his patience clearly exhausted. 'You do not approach Ben with any questions or demands. Not at all!' Simon emphasised as Gleeson started to object. 'He's just lost his parents and is only sixteen for Christ's sake. He can't make any decisions. The will reading is in a few weeks time and then we will all know how David and Helen's estate is to be taken care of, and that includes CordyGen. As for anything to do with company decisions I suggest that you take everything to the Board. I presume you can be classed as *acting* Director in Chief until you are either officially promoted…or someone else suitable is employed to do the job.'

Gleeson coughed, no doubt horrified at the thought that he might not simply take one step up the ladder and glide into David's position with no ripples of dissent. Behind the bookcase Ben suppressed a smile, knowing that Simon probably had as much idea as he had regarding how the company worked, but would be saying it for effect just to rankle Gleeson.

Gleeson started to raise an objection, but Simon cut across him. 'Like I said Charles this really isn't the time or the place. We'll know a lot more once the will has been read and the Board has been in session about putting into effect anything specific that Charles wanted to happen in the event of his death.' Ben heard the squeak as the door handle twisted, followed by the increase in volume as the door opened before dropping back to a murmur, and the click of the latch catching. He exhaled deeply letting his head fall back against the wall. He had no idea what was going to happen to him and knew that when his parents' wills were read his entire life as he knew it could be ripped apart more than it already was now.

Chapter 3

Ben Weir felt very small as he sat silently in the solicitor's office in a side street just off Queens Square. He kept his hands in front of him on the large, polished meeting table and stared at the spot between his two thumbs.   The solicitor's voice had receded into the background as thoughts of his parents crowded into his head. He still couldn't believe they were gone, both together.   He gritted his teeth and swallowed hard fighting back tears; he would not let them come in this setting.   He lifted his head and looked at the other people sat around the table.

Uncle Simon, sat on one side, was fiddling with his fingers, clearly as uncomfortable as Ben. Ben's father was the older brother; they had always had a strong bond, albeit not having a huge amount of contact with each other since they had grown up and embarked on their separate careers. David's in science and Simon's in…in what exactly? All Ben knew was that Uncle Simon was great fun, a textbook uncle, never missed birthdays or Christmas, but was rarely present in person. He didn't talk about his job and was often not in the country. He seemed to lead a solitary life. Ben's parents always joked that Simon was so in love with his career that no woman ever stood a chance. David always jokingly maintained that his younger brother was up to no good, and that his job was clearly something dodgy. As far as Simon was concerned his job simply wasn't a topic for polite conversation.

Ben looked over to the other side of the table. Aunt Evelyn and her husband sat alert, hanging on everything the solicitor was saying. They reminded Ben of hungry birds waiting to see what would drop their way. Evelyn was Helen's sister and Ben had never felt close to her. She was cold and bitter, so different from the warmth and fun that was his mother. Ben's mother would half joke that Evelyn was jealous. Evelyn's own husband had never aspired to anything. He was a 'cup half empty' sort of guy; Ben and his father would laugh about the dark cloud that must always hover over his baldhead. The world had done him a great disservice by not handing him a life of wealth and achievement on a plate. He didn't seem to realise that David and Simon Weir had achieved the lifestyles they had through sheer hard work and dedication. The result of this was that the Weir household went into decline when it was announced that Evelyn was paying a visit. Ben would find excuses as soon as possible to disappear up to his room. His mother always made him be present for the first cup of tea and slice of cake, that was the agreement between them; polite, stilted conversation over Ben would be off at the first opportunity.

He thought back to that fateful day almost exactly one month ago when the headmaster had come into the chemistry lab and spoken to Mr. Phillips asking for Ben to be excused. They had walked slowly back to the headmaster's study, neither speaking, Ben feeling pulled down with every step by the weight of something momentous he knew was coming. Uncle Simon stood up as soon as they entered the room. He had asked Ben to sit with him while the headmaster moved silently to the large bay window and looked out across the gardens and rugby fields beyond. Simon slowly explained to Ben that his parents were dead. Killed in a blast at his father's office. The cause was being investigated, but was not, as yet, known. Simon told Ben that the explosion was big; that they would not have known anything, and that he was so very sorry for Ben. It was at that point that Ben felt something fragile at his core shatter into a heap, along with the collapse came the tears.

The days straight after that meeting were a blur, as was the double funeral. Uncle Simon had taken Ben back home and stayed in the house with him, taken him out to buy a new black suit, the suit he was wearing in the solicitor's office now. Ben was led and pushed to various places, told to sit here or there. He listened to various people give eulogies or express their condolences to him. He shook hands, nodded, gazed into concerned faces and said 'Thank you' many times, but all of it on autopilot; the same autopilot that accompanied him into the solicitor's office.

'And now with the minor bequests and disbursements over, I come to Ben and the provision to be made for him in his parents' will, this does of course form the bulk of Professor and Dr Weir's wills.' At the sound of his name Ben started and looked into the face of the solicitor. The man hesitated for a moment peering over the half glasses that balanced on the end of his pointed nose and smiled pityingly at Ben before clearing his throat and focusing back on the document he held in his hands.

'The entire estate of Professor and Dr Weir is to be left in trust for Ben, the trustees being myself, Mr. Simon Weir and Mrs. Evelyn Appleby. Ben will be able to gain independent access to the trust on his 25th birthday, when our roles as trustees will cease to function. Yearly provision is to be made for Ben with regard to living expenses, school fees, and the running and maintenance of Luxborough House. As Ben is only just 16 and a minor he has been left the ward of his aunt, Evelyn Appleby and her husband.'

At the mention of Ben being left a ward of Evelyn, both Ben and his aunt took in a sharp breath and looked at each other, both surprised. Ben glared at Uncle Simon who, head bowed, was still examining his fingers in detail.

'Uncle Simon?' said Ben desperately. 'Uncle Simon please, you could live at home with Mrs. Jessop and me. You can be my guardian. I don't need another one.'

Simon slowly raised his head to look at Ben, his face a mask of concern. He knew he was letting Ben down. 'Ben, your mother and father discussed it with me, but I can't. I won't be around most of the time and you can't be left alone, not at 16. You know my work takes me away for long periods of time and sometimes I don't know when I will be coming back from trips. It's not going to happen.' Unable to meet Ben's imploring gaze any longer he looked back down at his fingers. Suddenly the air in the room had become heavy and thick.

'Well, they might have discussed it with me as well, but of course I am probably not important enough to be consulted. After all it might not be convenient for me either.' Aunt Evelyn's hard, high-pitched voice cut across the table as she glared at Simon.

'Oh don't worry Evelyn. I am sure everything will become convenient once you know exactly how much money you will be managing on an annual basis and of course you and Harry get to live in Luxborough House until Ben reaches the age of twenty five. So there are some perks.'

Before Evelyn could answer Simon back the solicitor interjected 'I would just like to point out here that the allocation of any monies will require agreement and consultation between all three of the trustees.'

Ben hated the way he was being talked about as if he wasn't there. He didn't want to be Evelyn's ward and if Uncle Simon didn't want him then he didn't want Uncle Simon either. Why couldn't he stay on his own, there was clearly enough money, he was a sensible lad and in term time he would be at school anyway? There was always Mrs. Jessop at Luxborough House, so he'd never really be on his own or responsible for himself. He felt a tidal wave of disappointment, anger, frustration and sorrow all rise at once in him. Unable to contain the pressure boiling inside him he jumped up suddenly from the table knocking his chair over and fled from the room.

Shaking off the stale confines of the solicitor's office and breathing in the fresh air Ben crossed the road to the park. He slumped heavily on a bench and put his head in his hands. He looked up and watched as a patient from the neurological hospital shuffled along in his dressing gown pulling a drip stand at the side of him. The man chose a bench in the sun and sat on the opposite side of the park to Ben, with some effort he lit a cigarette, and raised it to his lips with a trembling hand. Ben sat back feeling the wooden slats dig into him; he couldn't live with Evelyn, no way. What were his parents thinking of? Did they ever think this situation would really arise? Before he could let his mind race with thousands of questions, he felt someone sit on the bench next to him. They sat in silence for a few minutes before Simon spoke.

'You know it won't really be all that bad. You'll be away at school most of the time and I can make sure I take the holidays I am due and we can go away together. Evelyn can't make things too awful for you if you are not there a lot of the time. Plus Mrs. J will always be on your side.' Simon smiled at Ben trying, but failing, to get the same expression out of his nephew.

Ben looked at his uncle. 'Why did this have to happen? It was all so simple, all so good. Why did mum have to go to his office when she did? At least I would still have her.' Ben felt his voice crack and bit his bottom lip before his voice could betray him anymore.

'I don't have any answers Ben, but it's all being investigated. The truth will come out, but the explosion was probably due to an accident, a gas explosion of some sort. You know what laboratories are like, loads of flammable and explosive gases and liquids.' Ben felt the hair on his arms stand on end; there was something in Simon's voice that said that he possibly didn't quite believe his own words. Ben stared at the old man opposite who was nearing the end of his cigarette, his other hand still clutched to the drip stand.

'Come on we'd better get you back; it's a fair drive over to Luxborough House and I'd rather we got going before the rush hour starts. The A3 will be madness getting out of London if we leave it much later. I'll come in with you and we can explain to Mrs. J what's happening.'

Chapter 4

Ben buried himself in his schoolwork and the term raced by. Before he knew it, the exams he had worked so hard towards were over and it was time for him to pack up for the summer recess.

As the taxi left Leatherhead station Ben wondered what the summer was going to be like. Within a week of the will reading Aunt Evelyn and Uncle Harry had taken up residence in Luxborough House. He was glad to have had the excuse of going back to school to finish the summer term and do his GCSE exams. The less time he spent with his aunt and uncle the better. He hadn't heard anything from them while he'd been away, the only family letter he'd received was a short one from Uncle Simon asking how he was getting on and rallying him to concentrate on his exams and make the memory of his parents proud.

Ben slumped down into the car's back seat; his head leaning against the headrest as he watched the familiar sights pass by the window. He'd do anything to be anywhere else right now. Within a few minutes they were going down the hill, passing the church where his parents were buried. Ben resisted the temptation to look over.

The taxi passed through the iron gates and drew up alongside the front porch causing the gravel to crunch and scatter. The dark green door opened and the familiar form of Mrs. Jessop stepped out to welcome Ben home. Ben paid the driver and stepped out of the car into a bear hug, smelling the familiar scent of Mrs. J's bosom, a scent he'd smelt since childhood when he would crawl up onto her knee. As the taxi driver unloaded Ben's suitcases from the boot of the car Mrs. J held Ben at arms' length looking him up and down.

'Right young man, the first thing you need is a good feed. I don't know what those cooks at that school think they are doing but whatever it is it isn't enough of the good stuff that's for sure.' Ben smiled; at least she was just the same.

The taxi scattered more gravel as it drove around the patch of grass and disappeared down the drive. Mrs.

Jessop picked up one suitcase and Ben took the heavier one. As they entered the wide hallway a clipped shrill voice called out from the room that was his father's study.

'What was that car Mrs. Jessop?'

Mrs. J put the suitcase down heavily on the floor and stood up straight. Her face set, one eyebrow raised. 'It's Master Ben home for the summer holidays Madam.'

Ben looked at Mrs. J with horror and mouthed the word 'Madam?' Mrs. J rolled her eyes, her face turning back to a mask of impassiveness just as the study door was pulled fully open and the thin angular frame of Aunt Evelyn appeared. She marched over to Ben, her heels making a hard clicking sound on the stone flags. Ben looked at her awkwardly, her presence made him feel like a stranger in his own home. The home he was born in.

She smiled 'Welcome home Ben.' Except the words were devoid of any warmth and the smile stopped before it reached her eyes. 'Your room is still the same, we haven't decorated that one yet so you should find everything just as you left it.'

'What do you mean *you haven't decorated that one yet?*'

'Well, really Ben, you can't expect us to live in a house without having things the way we like it, and much as my sister had a brain for science it rather fell short in the field of artistic interiors. Remember, as much as this is still your house, it is also our house now.' She couldn't help keep the hint of smugness out of her voice.

Ben looked around the hall, his heart pounding with emotion. It looked just the same; perhaps one or two pictures had changed but nothing that struck him immediately. He pushed past his aunt and marched to his father's study. Two steps into the room he was brought up short, he looked around in horror. Every trace of his father had been removed. The walls of bookcases with shelves groaning under the weight of academic books had gone, replaced with white low sideboards and angular occasional tables. The walls had been painted a pale grey, the sort of colour you would see in a railway station waiting room. The atmosphere smelt fresh, perfumed, not the smell of books, stale air and dust…not the smell of his father. Most importantly his father's desk, the big heavy desk made of oak with a dark red leather inlay on its surface was missing. In its place was a long three-man settee of pale grey and white damask material.

Ben turned as he heard Aunt Evelyn come in behind him; his arms were rigid by his sides, fists clenched. He didn't think he had ever felt such fury as he did right now. Aunt Evelyn beamed, 'Well I hope you like it? So much lighter and welcoming now with all those dusty books and heavy furniture gone.'

'Where are they?' Ben growled through gritted teeth.

'Where are what?' Aunt Evelyn asked innocently, the smile just starting to fade.

'My father's things? His books? The bookcases? His desk?' With each word Ben's voice became more and more stern.

'I don't think I like your tone Benjamin! Remember you are under my care now and you will treat me with respect.'

'And I don't like what you have done while I have been at school, you had no right to change anything. These things belonged to my parents and they belong to me now, not you, me! This is my house not yours…and don't call me Benjamin!'

'Well really Ben, you are not the adult here. We are the adults who have been given the task of taking care of you. We are now your guardians and we are responsible for you. That means that there has to be compromise on both our parts and I for one can't live in a mausoleum to your parents. They are gone Ben, we are still here.'

The stark reality of her words crushed Ben and drew the fire out of his anger. 'Where are the books and the things from my father's desk?' he asked quietly, his eyes refusing to meet his aunt's.

'That's better! They are all in boxes in the attic. The book cases have already been collected by a local charity and the desk is in the garage awaiting collection tomorrow.' Evelyn pulled the cardigan draped across her shoulders tighter as if taking courage from its embrace. Ben pushed passed his aunt and picking up his suitcases started up the stairs to his room at the top of the house. The two women watched him from the hallway.

'I told you, you should have held off doing anything until he'd come home from school and you could discuss it.' Mrs. J said sharply to Evelyn.

'And I have told you before now that none of this is any of your business. You are here to cook, fetch and clean. Don't think I haven't noticed your sarcastic comments and looks; so far I have chosen to ignore them. We all need to get used to things, but believe me when I tell you Mrs. Jessop that I will not put up with them forever. My sister is no longer in charge of this house, I am. I will thank you to attend to your duties and keep your opinions to yourself.'

Ben ignored the war of words between the two women. He'd never looked so much to the start of the new school year as he did that minute…and the school holidays had only just begun.

Chapter 5

The next few days were a trial until Ben and his aunt had managed to work out an unspoken routine for keeping out of each other's way. He had successfully managed to stave off attempts by the charity men to collect his father's desk and Evelyn had reluctantly agreed to let it sit in the garage for now. One saving grace was that at least Evelyn had had the good sense to leave his parents' bedroom alone. Over tea and apple cake one afternoon Mrs. J told Ben how she had gone through Ben's parents' clothes before Evelyn could make a start on them. Other than that everything remained in its place and when he felt up to it he could go in there and decide what he wanted to do with things. Ben thanked her and then put the existence of the room from his mind; so long as Evelyn kept her fingers off it he was happy to leave it as it was for now. He didn't feel that he was ready to face it.

The morning had gone well. Ben had amused himself with several laps of the orchard on his 50cc Suzuki off road bike. He took pleasure in the thought that somewhere on the house Evelyn would be able to hear the high whine of the bike's engine but would be reluctant to walk down to the orchard to stop him. He set himself various routes dodging between the fruit trees and tried to beat his own times. It was only the arrival of Mrs. J with a welcome piece of pork pie, some sandwiches and a jug of iced juice that got him out of the saddle.

After lunch Ben decided to go for a walk. He followed the public footpath along the river keeping an eye out for a sudden flash of bright blue and orange that would signify the flight of a kingfisher. He'd never managed to spot one of the little birds while it was sat in the reeds or trees that over hung the river, but the reward of that sudden splash of colour was all he needed to know the birds were still about. Across the fields he cut up right into Norbury Park and followed the bridle path until he came to a wild flower meadow. The plants were in full swing and the meadow was a blaze of many different species of butterfly; as a younger child he had come up here with his net and caught them, keeping notes of all the species he could find. He felt a tongue of sadness lick at him as he remembered that. How many of these fabulous insects had he inadvertently killed in his ham-fisted attempt at catching them and handling them while he checked his butterfly guidebook?

Ben stopped a moment and watched a large peacock butterfly as it sipped at the flowers of a pale mauve field scabious. Its wings slowly opening and closing, showing the large eye markings as it probed the small florets with its long tongue. For a brief second a wave of grief hit him like a sledgehammer. His eyes brimmed and he felt hot tears run down his cheeks. The butterfly blurred from view. He took in a few deep, rasping breaths that made his chest shake before he managed to control himself. So many people had told him that he must just let go and get it all out of his system, but he couldn't. Getting it out of his system meant moving on and moving on meant moving further from his parents.

For now keeping their memory as strong as possible, no matter how painful, was all he had to cling onto.

Ben looked at his watch and decided he'd better start to head back home. He followed the path that would take him in a big loop down to the river and then back home to Luxborough House. As he let himself through the side gate he heard raised voices, Mrs. J and his aunt were still at it. Following the voices Ben walked around to the front garden just in time to see Aunt Evelyn turn on her heel and march back into the house slamming the front door after her. Mrs. J stood ramrod straight with her back to the house staring down the drive. She had her coat on and her hands were clasped tightly at her waist. To Ben's horror a large blue suitcase sat on the gravel next to her. He burst into a run, the sound of his feet on the gravel causing Mrs. Jessop to turn. Her face relaxed from a mask of anger to one of sadness, her eyes brimmed and her chin wobbled.

'Oh master Ben! I never thought it would come to this. I am so sorry, I can't stand another moment of being in this house with that woman.'

'She can't fire you or throw you out, not without my say so. The will states that.' Ben, fists bunched made to run into the house to confront his aunt, but Mrs. J caught his wrist.

'No Ben,' she said gravely. He knew it was serious because she was speaking to him as an equal and had dropped the 'master'. 'I've given my notice with immediate effect. There's a letter inside for you. I'll not change my mind and I am so sorry to leave you, but I can't bear to be in her presence a minute longer while she lords it over everyone and bit-by-bit tries to erase your mother and father. You need to be firm Ben or she'll have this entire place to her own whim. Your parents rubbed away like that.' She snapped her fingers hard. 'I'm waiting for a taxi to pick me up, I'll be off to my sister's in Putney and I'll send for the rest of my stuff. It's already packed up in my room so whoever comes will just have to pick up the boxes.'

'But there's no need for this, look let me speak to her. She can't do this.'

Mrs. J held up her hand, 'She's not doing anything other than the obvious Ben; it's my decision to leave.

It's either that or so help me God I will swing for her one of these days. You have all my contact details in the letter and you are welcome to come and see me anytime you want to. It would be a pleasure for me.'

'But you can't go,' Ben implored her, 'You've been here forever, since just after I was born. Please...' Ben looked down at his feet, 'I can't lose you too, not after mum and dad.'

Mrs. Jessop pulled Ben to her and hugged him tightly. Ben threw his arms around her and held on. This was all too much. He opened his eyes and saw a pinch faced, thin frame looking at them through the drawing room window. His grief gave way to a sudden burst of anger. Pulling away from Mrs. J, Ben stepped towards the door. 'I'll sort this out now. Don't go anywhere. You belong here and not her or her husband. I don't care if she is my aunt, she won't get away with anything anymore.'

Mrs. Jessop called after Ben, but the heavy wooden door closing behind his retreating form cut off her words. She took a small white handkerchief from her coat pocket and wiped her eyes before stooping to pick up her suitcase. With a heavy heart and a boiling mass of emotions in her breast she walked slowly down the drive.

'What the hell do you think you are doing?' shouted Ben before he had even entered the drawing room. 'You have no right to come in here and start changing things. No right to get rid of my parents' things. No right to force Mrs. Jessop out. You are the one who should go. You do not belong here!' Aunt Evelyn had retreated to stand by the fireplace and looked stunned by Ben's onslaught, but it didn't take long for the flinty gleam to return to her eyes.

'Just who do you think you are talking to Ben. I am your aunt. Your mother's sister and also your appointed guardian. Appointed by your parents of their own free will. They clearly considered that I would have your best interests at heart and take care of you, as they would have wanted. I didn't ask for this task, but I have risen to their wish. Which is more than can be said for your father's brother! Where's he in all this?'

'Oh don't worry, I ask myself the same questions. I'd rather he was here than you. Things would be a lot more fun…and things would be pretty much the same too.' Ben was shaking; all the emotions of the last few weeks were coming to the surface but in anger. He could feel the heat in his cheeks and knew he would be red faced, a direct contrast to the ice that seemed to flow through Aunt Evelyn. Stepping away from the fireplace she drew herself up standing very erect and marched towards Ben. Her heels clicking on the parquet flooring.

'I'll give you the benefit of the doubt after what you have been through,' she said, her voice clipped, the thin veneer of trying to sound genuine failing to hide the patronizing note. 'However, I will not tolerate another outburst like this. Nobody can change what has happened and I will not have you screaming and shouting at me when we all have to get along under this roof.'

Ben opened his mouth to challenge her but Evelyn held up a hand sharply in front of his face. 'Anymore of this nonsense and I will be writing to the solicitor, and your Uncle Simon, with regard to reviewing the terms of your allowance.' With that she strode out of the drawing room and disappeared down the hall towards the back of the house. Ben, his fists balled tightly, let out a shout of frustration and muttered a curse at his parents for having left him in this situation. A curse he instantly felt guilty for having said. He remembered Mrs. J and went outside with the intention of taking her suitcase from her and bringing it back inside.

As Ben opened the heavy front door he looked out from the colonnaded portico into the empty space of the graveled driveway and round grass island. Mrs. J had gone. Ben swore and took off at a run down the drive and over the narrow river bridge to the main road. He stood and looked both ways but there was no sign of his former nanny. After a moment's hesitation he turned and ran back to the house, straight up to his room. Slamming the door behind him he sat down heavily in the chair at his desk and hit the button to bring his laptop back to life.

After ten minutes he stopped and reread the email he had constructed to his Uncle Simon. He altered a couple of sentences that referred to his Aunt Evelyn in less than glowing terms and tried to tone down the language, but not the thrust of his message. As far as he was concerned the whole situation really couldn't go on and his threat to leave Luxborough House was very serious in his own mind. Once he was satisfied and sure the wording would get Simon's attention he hit send.

For a few seconds Ben stared at the screen, fixing on the small box in the centre of the monitor telling him his email had been sent successfully. If Simon didn't respond he didn't know what he was going to do. He'd put some pretty strong ultimatums in the email and wasn't sure if he could carry them out if his uncle called his bluff.

He got up and opened his bedroom door listening for any sign of his aunt or uncle. When he was sure it was safe to venture forth he crossed the landing and made his way to his parents' bedroom. He hesitated for a moment, his hand on the door handle. With a deep breath he pushed the handle down and walked in.

He could still smell the faint scent of his mother's perfume on the air. She would have put some on before setting off into London to meet with his father. He walked over to the bookcase and looked at the spines.

They were a mix of his father's non-fiction tastes; mostly biology, wildlife or environmentally related and his mother's fiction; romance and chick lit. They were the books his father always made fun of her for reading, but secretly loved, as it showed she hadn't lost her sense of romance after all the years they had been married. Ben swallowed back the lump in his throat as he stroked a finger along several of the titles.

He looked slowly around the room; their dressing gowns from behind the door were gone. The chair that always had some garment draped over it waiting to be put in the wash or hung up properly was bare...another stark reminder.

Lost in his thoughts Ben jumped as he heard a muted knock on his own bedroom door, followed by his name. His Uncle Harry, no doubt coming to have a 'fatherly' chat with him about how he had spoken to his aunt. Ben supposed Uncle Harry was okay, harmless. He was just characterless, rarely spoke and when he did it was often something unrelated or inappropriate to the topic of conversation. Ben froze, not trusting the floorboards to give him away. In the silence his own heartbeat echoed in his ears. He heard his uncle knock again and when there was no answer Harry called that they could perhaps talk in the morning. Ben heard his footsteps recede down the stairs. He sat on the end of his parents' bed for a few minutes before picking up his mother's perfume bottle from the dressing table and, tucking it into his pocket, took it back to his room.

Chapter 6

As Ben stood under the hot shower letting the water play over his neck and shoulders he considered his situation. Since his big bust up with Aunt Evelyn he had managed to avoid both her and his uncle successfully. It wasn't too difficult as he sensed they were just as keen to avoid him as he was them. He'd spent yesterday in London doing the rounds of a couple of the bigger museums, stretching out the stay until the last one closed for the day, then he headed to the Pizza Express in Waterloo. He felt a bit odd sitting on his own, but at least he wouldn't have to sit with them around the dinner table. One of the drawbacks of going to a boarding school miles away from home is that when you're back for the holidays there are no local friends to do things with.

There had been no response from Uncle Simon and Ben weighed up whether or not he should send another email. He didn't want to sound too desperate or needy but at the same time he didn't want to just sit and wait.

Reluctantly he turned off the shower and while he was toweling himself down he heard raised voices drifting up from downstairs. Wrapping the towel around his waist he stuck his head round the bathroom door. He heard the shrill tones of Aunt Evelyn barely drawing breath, no doubt haranguing her husband for something or other. She was cut short by a man's voice, deep and stern; the sort of voice that commanded respect and you were compelled to listen to. That certainly wasn't Harry; he wouldn't dare answer her back.

Ben's heart skipped a beat as he recognized the voice. Uncle Simon. He was downstairs and it sounded like he was reading the riot act to Evelyn. Ben raced across the landing to his room and dressed as quickly as he could. A few minutes later he carefully made his way down the staircase. He knew exactly where every creaky board was and placed his feet carefully, skillfully avoiding any sounds that would give him away. He stopped on the last step and craned his neck towards his father's study door. Simon was berating

Evelyn for not working with Mrs. Jessop and making things so awful that she felt she had to leave. Harry tried to cut in to defend his wife but Simon silenced him immediately. Ben could imagine Harry sinking back into the chair he was sat in hoping to become as nondescript and unnoticed as one of Evelyn's bland cushions. Evelyn saw her chance and started on again, her voice becoming more strident. She was having a go at Ben now saying how unappreciative he was, how he was difficult and rebellious and needed a firm hand to take control of him, she then progressed to very dangerous waters by berating Simon about not taking his share of responsibility for Ben.

Although he wasn't in the room Ben could feel his heart racing, his own adrenaline surge kicking in from the energy of the argument. Silently he was cheering his Uncle Simon on. His saviour come to beard the dragon in her den. His heart almost stopped dead when he heard his name called out.

'Ben! I said come in here now. There's no point standing out there listening, this is as much your business as it is ours.' Uncle Simon's voice left Ben in no doubt that he was in no mood for any messing about.

Ben walked into his father's study, his cheeks flushing red as all faces turned to him. Simon was sat back on the new settee, if Ben hadn't heard some of the heated exchanges he would have sworn his uncle was enjoying himself. Evelyn sat ramrod straight on one of his parents' dining chairs that had been set against the wall. She had been crying, another one of the tools in her performance box when she wasn't getting her own way. Ben's mental image of his Uncle Harry was correct; he was sitting in one of the wing chairs that flanked the fireplace, pushed as far back into the chair as he could. He was the first to look away as Ben's gaze met every face in the room.

'Well I gather you know what this is all about, you've been stood there long enough.' Ben was about to object, but Simon held his hand up. 'It is quite clear that things are going to have to change around here and that the current set up is not working…for everybody concerned.' Simon looked at the other two, Harry was still studying the trouser material covering his knees, but Evelyn was glaring at Simon. If looks could kill he'd have expired in that instant. 'So what I propose is that in the first instance we put some time and distance between your good selves and Ben here.' Ben and Evelyn both started to speak at once, but Simon silenced them.

'Ben, I want you to go upstairs and pack enough summer clothes and books and anything else you need to keep you entertained for a five week period. Evelyn, I'm taking Ben away for a few weeks, God knows he deserves some fun after all he's been through. During that time you do not carry out anymore decorating or changes to the house. You can think how this situation might be improved while we're away and we will do the same, so that by the time Ben comes home we will have something sensible to discuss about how we go forward from here.' Simon turned to look at Ben who was stood doing goldfish impressions after the shock of his uncle's words. 'Well go on then lad, we need to leave soon if we're to catch the plane...and make sure you've got your passport!'

Ben didn't need telling twice. He had no idea what his uncle was up to, but if it meant some time away from Luxborough House and time with him then he was definitely ready for it. He raced upstairs and pulled the suitcase from the top of his wardrobe not caring that it hit the floor with a massive thud. He packed as many pairs of shorts and t-shirts as he could into it, followed by some long trousers and a couple of long sleeved shirts and a jumper just in case; this was all followed by swimming things, some running gear, two pairs of flip flops and his toiletry bag. Without missing a beat Ben grabbed his small rucksack and loaded it with his headphones, wallet, passport, phone charger and some books.

'You all set?' Simon asked as Ben burst breathless into the room.

'All packed.' Ben slapped the front pouch of his rucksack, 'Passport too.'

'I guess we better get started then.' Simon stood up and brushed the creases out of his jeans. 'I'll let you know when we get there and keep you informed of what we are up to,' he said formally to Evelyn and

Harry who had both stood up too. It was clear the meeting was at an end, more of an impasse reached than a solution for now, but Ben didn't care about that. He was getting away from here and spending time with his uncle.

Ben hurried out of the house as if wanting to get on his way before Simon might consider he'd made a mistake. He loaded the case into the back of Simon's black BMW X5 and threw his rucksack on top of it. He was just reaching for the passenger door handle when Simon called him. 'Don't you think you should at least say "Goodbye?"'

Ben blushed at his thoughtlessness, no matter what, Evelyn and Harry were still his aunt and uncle and if his parents were here they would have admonished him for such tardy lack of respect. Evelyn still hadn't said much since Simon had unveiled his plan. She stood ramrod stiff, her hands clasped together in front of her, lips pursed and cheeks sucked in. As Ben moved towards her she remained silent, turning a cold cheek for him to kiss, Ben shook hands with Harry who smiled and told him to have a good time. Ben retreated to the car as soon as he could, and after a few minutes of conversation he could not hear, Simon joined him in the driving seat.

They were soon zooming down the M25 to Gatwick airport with the windows down, Ben felt as if the wind was blowing away all the bad feelings that had been wrapping around him like a tightening spider's web. Simon quickly made the rule that there was to be no mention of Luxborough House, Aunt Evelyn or even Mrs Jessop while they were away. He refused to tell Ben their destination saying the suspense of the journey would add to the thrill of the holiday. He was right too, Ben kept guessing, racking his brains to think of all the places he'd heard Simon mention or places he had said himself that he would like to visit. Every guess was met with a shake of Simon's head or a negative. It was only when they were sat in the waiting lounge for their flight that Ben twigged they were bound for Nice airport, but even then the mystery continued because Simon added they needed to jump in a taxi to Nice Ville station and catch a train.

'Come on, this is us.' Simon said standing up and stretching. Ben had tried to listen to the announcements of the stations on the train, but as they were all in French and then switched to Italian he had given up. Instead he watched the changing scenery as the train hugged the coast and travelled from Nice, through Monte Carlo, over the border into Italy via Ventimiglia and then on. Simon was clearly familiar with the route, since he pointed out various aspects of the coast and seemed to have no problem with speaking either French or Italian. Ben had got the gist of conversations in the former but it wasn't one of his best subjects at school, the Italian however completely flummoxed him.

Stepping off the train onto the platform the first thing Ben noticed was the heat, the train had been air-conditioned and it was now mid-afternoon. The second thing he spotted was the town's name, Alassio.

'This way,' said Simon like a tour guide, he was clearly familiar with the station lay out. In the forecourt Simon walked over to the taxi rank and spoke to one of the drivers, then he beckoned Ben over as the driver got out and popped the boot for their suitcases.

'So where are we then?' asked Ben once the taxi had pulled out into traffic.

'We're in a lovely Italian Riviera town called Alassio, behind us is Monte Carlo and France as you know and if we carried on we would end up in either Genoa or Milan. This bit of Italy is known as the Ligurian coast and I'm pretty sure you'll like it.'

'It's a lot better than being at Lux…'

'Hold it! We had that agreement in the car remember.'

Ben blushed and then beamed. 'You got it. No LH talk while we're here.'

Simon held his hand up in a high five, although Ben thought it was a bit corny and his uncle was trying just a bit too hard to 'get it on', he still high fived him back. The taxi started to climb up a steep winding road and Ben wound his window down as far as it would go. Sticking his head out of the window he looked back and could see the main part of the town leading down to the sea behind him. Mostly sandy coloured buildings with terracotta tiled roofs and various colours of wooden shutters that were closed over their windows to keep the heat out.

Simon chatted to the taxi driver in Italian and it wasn't too long before the taxi pulled up alongside tall electric gates. Ben couldn't see what lay behind them as the drive curved and a mix of tall bushy oleanders and some plants he didn't recognise obscured the view. His uncle paid the taxi driver and the two stood in front of the gates. Simon fished a small black object that looked a little like a USB stick out of his pocket and pointed it at a discreet metal box screwed to the gatepost. The gates swung open smoothly without a sound and the two walked down the drive.

Ben stopped, his jaw hanging open. 'Blimey Uncle Simon! What is this place?' They stood in front of a large three story white villa. Dark green shutters were tightly closed over the windows; small louvered sections in each shutter were propped open to allow a fresh airflow. The gardens were manicured and well looked after and around the side the building Ben could just see the blue and reflected ripples of sunlight off what could only be a swimming pool.

Simon laughed, 'Oh don't worry. It isn't mine. It belongs to work and they let people use it now and again, well they let me use it now and again. So, treat it like home for the next few weeks.'

Ben didn't know whether to believe him or not. It was clear that Simon had been here many times; he spoke the language, had the route sorted and knew the layout of the town like a regular. Whatever, it all added to the mystery of what Simon Weir was about. Ben caught Simon up at the front door and followed his uncle into a wide and airy vestibule. The floor and skirting boards were made of white marble and everything was clean, as if the owner had just stepped out to go into town for a moment.

Simon threw his keys down on a hall table and gave Ben the run down. 'Kitchen's over there, two living rooms there and there. You've terraces on all three sides so you can chase the sun round during the day if you want to. Downstairs loo and shower room, handy for when you're using the pool…and no peeing in it, the pool that is! Think that's about it for this level. Let me show you upstairs.'

Ben couldn't believe his eyes, even with his parents being quite well off they had never stayed in a place like this, besides his dad was almost married to his work so he often cut holidays short to get back to his laboratory.

A central marble staircase led up to the upper levels. 'That's my room. And you have the choice of any of these three, they've all got their own en suites.'

'No expense spared eh? What's that room?'

'Ah that room I am afraid is out of bounds. It's a workroom, a study if you like and the company has some sensitive equipment and what have you in there so it's always locked. Treat the place as your own and go anywhere you like but just avoid that one…and that's not an invitation for you to try and see what's in there!'

Ben laughed, 'No worries, there's plenty to keep me occupied without wondering about that.'

'Right, have a look in the rooms and choose which you want, it really doesn't matter which one. I'm off to unpack and shower and then how about some late lunch? Camilla should have left us plenty of food to rustle something up. You'll probably be meeting her tomorrow morning.'

Simon disappeared into his room with his luggage and left Ben to explore. He chose the room that overlooked the pool. It was large with a balcony all down one side. The large windows were shaded with an awning and it felt like the coolest of the rooms on offer. After unpacking and showering Ben wandered downstairs and followed the sounds to the kitchen where he found Simon preparing a salad and some cold chicken.

While they ate a leisurely lunch on the poolside terrace, Ben asked Simon about the town and surrounding area and what sort of things there were to do. It was mostly walking up in the hills, chilling and exploring the town from what Ben could work out. Simon explained where the tennis club was and also the running track. For the moment Ben was okay with just kicking back and it was a good chance to get to know his uncle more. He'd always had a good rapport with him, but he constantly had a sense that there was something more beneath the surface; another part of

Simon that was always held back. Ben listened intently as Simon explained a little about the town's history. How at the end of the nineteenth century and beginning of the twentieth it was a haven for English tourists who not only visited but also settled there, but now it was the place where the Italians went on holiday, especially coming down from Milan and Turin. Not finished with the surprises Simon also told Ben that he had something good planned for the third week of their stay, but Ben had to go to school first.

'School, what do you mean school? I thought you'd brought me here to get away from things, to chill out and have a great time.'

Simon laughed at his nephew's reaction and horror stricken face. 'Don't worry, I think you'll like this school, it's a bit different.'

'Really?' Ben didn't sound convinced, his chin dropping to the floor.

Chapter 7

On their first morning Simon introduced Ben to Camilla who came in each day and acted as the housekeeper, tidying the beds and keeping the place clean. She was a very smiley, stout 60 something who tried very hard to speak to Ben in stilted English, which he appreciated. He tried not to think of parallels with Mrs Jessop. If Simon was around then he acted as interpreter for them if necessary.

Ben also met Franco. He was a little bit older than Ben and was hired to keep the gardens looking good and to maintain the pool. He would arrive early and leave late, his comings and goings broadcast by the high-pitched whine of his Vespa scooter. Most mornings when Ben opened the shutters to his bedroom he would look down from the balcony and there was Franco with a large net skimming leaves and other floating debris from the surface of the pool. Simon explained that he'd arrived in Italy a few years back as a refugee from North Africa, probably Libya, a former colony of the Italian Empire. They didn't know much about his background other than his family had been killed in one of the many conflicts there, and he had managed to get himself across the Mediterranean on one of the barely floating, overcrowded boats that appeared all too often on the television. Franco didn't speak any English and every attempt by Ben to engage with him in some way was met with a beaming smile and rapid nodding of his head. One day Ben tried to gesture that Franco could have a swim in the pool if he wanted, after all he was the one cleaning it everyday. But once Franco had stopped nodding his head and realised what Ben was offering, he quickly put up a hand in protest and shook his head, his broad grin disappearing.

Ben and his uncle's first few days were spent exploring the town. One day they walked lazily along the beach from the far side of Alassio to the much smaller town of Laigueglia. Where Alassio had some more commercial areas and boutique shopping streets,

Laigueglia was the opposite. Pretty much untouched by the previous century and much sleepier. On the return journey neither of them could resist the warmth of the sea as it lapped over their bare feet, and after a quick change into their swimming trunks, larked about in the surf.

When they weren't down in the town Ben spent most of his time in the pool or reading. At first his mind constantly wandered back and forth between his parents and what might be going on back at home, but as his body relaxed into the holiday so did his mind.

The following Monday morning Ben was awoken early by a knocking on his bedroom door, peering over the sheet, eyes barely open he saw Simon's head poking around the door at him. 'Glad to see you're awake; come on, early start today! You need some breakfast and then it's off to school with you. Oh and pack your swimming gear.'

'What?' Ben groaned, sleepily rubbing one of his eyes, but when he refocused on the door Simon had gone.

Rushing through a light breakfast Ben met his uncle at the front of the house. 'Where did that come from?' Ben pointed at the silver soft-top Audi TT.

'You didn't notice the garage then?' Simon gestured from the driver's seat. Ben peered around the other side of the building and saw the garage tucked away towards the back of the house. He couldn't believe he hadn't spotted it. The doors were still propped open and he could see two scooters. He recognized Franco's battered pale green Vespa, but the shiny black one was new to him.

Throwing his rucksack onto the back seat he got in the car. 'You know, if this is a real school you're dumping me in so that you can go off and enjoy yourself and not baby sit me, I'll think of something suitably rebellious to do as an objection.'

'Well I think if you're going to be here for several weeks you should really get to grips with the language.'

'What?' said Ben as the car pulled quickly away from the villa and down the steep winding road. He spent the journey in brooding silence, while Simon grinned and chuckled to himself amused at his own joke.

They weren't on the road for long before Simon pulled into the marina on the far eastern side of the town. 'Here we are.'

Ben's brow furrowed as he looked around confused. All he could see were small fishing boats and large expensive yachts. He spotted a sign indicating the harbour master's office, another for a café and one for a toilet block, but that was it, no language school.

'Come on then, we don't want to be late on your first day.' Ben pulled a face back at his uncle.

'*Avanti subito!*' Simon commanded with a flourish of his arms.

Ben got out of the car hesitantly, not quite sure what was going on. 'Here, catch!' Simon shouted as he launched something dark grey, which Ben caught almost as a reflex action as it hurtled towards him.

'A wetsuit?'

'Well do you want to learn how to dive or not?' Simon replied as he grinned from ear to ear and pulled his own wetsuit from the car's boot.

'You're kidding. Really?' A wave of combined excitement and relief flooded through Ben. 'You bet.' Any reluctance to attend school had suddenly evaporated as fast as the early morning clouds once the sun got going. He hurried on to catch up with Simon who was marching to the far end of the marina where Ben could see a small crowd of people.

After a bit of an introduction in English and Italian about how things worked and a run through safety instructions, the teacher sent everybody off to get changed into their swimwear and wet suits. They reconvened back on one of the pontoons. A wave of sadness hit Ben unexpectedly as he watched a guy about his age whose parents were fussing over him. The boy was trying to downplay the concern his mother in particular was expressing. He looked furtively left and right checking out if anyone else had noticed. Eventually, with instructions that they would be waiting for him in the marina café, they departed leaving him alone.

The boat took them to just the other side of the breakwater wall where they were given instructions about how the mouthpieces, masks and cylinders worked. That first day though they were just being shown how to dive using snorkels to get them used to the water and breathing with a mouthpiece. Before they got in the water the instructor told them to get in pairs. Ben turned to Simon, but his uncle had other ideas. 'Sorry mate but I'm ducking out of this one.'

'How do you mean?' asked Ben.

'I've been diving for years and don't need to attend school. I'm just here for the ride and to make sure you don't get yourself into trouble.'

Ben raised his eyebrows, but guessed he shouldn't be that surprised; was there anything Simon hadn't done? 'So what am I supposed to do?'

Ben looked around the boat; virtually everybody else seemed to have been a pair of some sort in the first place, family members or friends. Then he spied the boy who was being fussed over by his mother. He was sat alone making a concerted effort checking the snorkel he'd been given. It was the sort of thing Ben would normally have done, wanting someone to approach him and not having the confidence to approach someone else.

Ben stood up and left Simon putting on his oxygen cylinder. He walked down the deck of the boat. 'Hey, I'm Ben,' he said, trying to sound cool and confident. 'You're English aren't you?'

The other lad lifted his head, 'Yeah I am.'

'Wanna pair up then? Seems we're the only English two on our own.'

'Thought you were with that other guy down there?'

'Well I am, but not for this. He can already dive. He's my uncle.'

'Oh right. Well I guess it's you and me then.' A smile flickered across his freckled face. Ben thought that he had confidence problems at times, but this guy was hard work.

'I'm Ben,' he said again. 'Ben Weir.'

'Oh yeah, right. Richard Osborne'

The instructor called them all to attention. Looking up Ben saw Simon sat on the edge of the boat, tank on his back and mask in place. He waved at Ben and then leant back disappearing in a splash.

Ben felt like the morning had evaporated when the instructor blew his whistle and called everyone back into the boat. Simon had surfaced a couple of times and Ben had watched underwater when Simon dived eventually disappearing from view when the light couldn't really penetrate any further. He'd give anything to be able to do that and feel the freedom of having all that water around him. Ben and Richard got to know each other a bit more and had a laugh as well as learning how to snorkel, use hand signals and practicing short shallow dives. On the journey back to the marina Ben and Richard chatted easily. Without them realising Simon watched from the other side of the boat and was glad that Ben had found someone he could perhaps hang around with. Especially since he needed to focus on the real reason he'd come to Alassio. It would be a lot easier if Ben had a distraction.

When they docked Richard's parents were waiting on the pontoon, clearly too impatient to wait in the café. His mother enthusiastically welcomed her son like he'd been away at sea for months, never mind a few hours. Simon walked Ben over to the family and introduced himself and Ben saying how much his nephew had enjoyed Richard's company. Mr. and Mrs. Osborne had only been in Alassio a few days but they were booked to stay for nearly three weeks before going off to Menton for another week and then back home to London. Like Ben, Richard was also signed up for the diving school that week. Simon felt a wave of relief at the thought that Ben could invite Richard up to the pool at the villa and also that he had a buddy for the diving school. Simon explained their situation to the Osbornes and said Richard was welcome to visit the villa. With 'Goodbyes' said and agreements to meet the following morning, Ben and Simon got changed and drove on to the next town for lunch.

The week passed quickly and by the end of the course both Ben and Richard received first level certificates for shallow diving with tanks. Simon announced that he had organized a surprise for Ben the following week and that Richard was welcome to join them if the Osbornes could be at the harbour for 9 o'clock. Richard's dad looked relieved that his son had a distraction to take him away from his mother. He had said as much to Simon as an aside. He was their only child, but now he was 16 he was becoming a young man and his mother needed to start letting go. Simon agreed, as if he had a wealth of parental experience to draw on.

All weekend Ben had pestered his uncle about Monday's surprise but he couldn't get anything out of him. He'd been left to his own devices for a fair amount of time. Once, when he thought his uncle had gone out and being on his own all morning with just Camilla and Franco for company, he caught Simon coming out of the company office room. When his uncle realised Ben had seen him he apologised for being engrossed in work. Ignoring all Ben's attempts to find out what he had been doing in there, he did his usual side step, suggesting the pool and the need to swim and stretch after sitting for a long time.

Monday morning quickly came around and the Osbornes were waiting down at the marina as agreed. Simon gave his assurances that he would have Richard back by 5pm and that his parents needn't worry but go off and enjoy themselves. Simon handed out diving equipment and food and drink supplies to both boys. Then, like the pied piper leading a much-diminished flock, he led the two loaded up teenagers down a pontoon to a waiting yacht. The boys couldn't believe their eyes or their luck. Simon told them that he wanted to take them diving and knew some shallow reefs that were perfect for the job. Just when they thought it couldn't get better he informed them that he'd hired the yacht for the week so they could, if they wanted to, go out each day. He'd barely finished his sentence before the boys, beaming from ear to ear, were shouting their agreement to the idea.

Ben was given the job of casting off from the pontoon and then joined Richard at the bow of the vessel as it journeyed out of the marina and into the bay. Before long it was clear that they were heading to an island off the coast of Alassio. Ben had asked about it before and Simon had told him that it was called Isola di Gallinara, Island of the Birds. Centuries ago it was home to monks, but now it was a protected nature reserve with special licenses required to land there or dive on its reefs. Ben had listened attentively but the one thing he couldn't get out of his mind was that the island's profile looked like some giant sea turtle slowly paddling through the surf, its head and neck extending from the hump of its shell.

As the island loomed larger, Ben relayed the information to Richard. Simon steered the yacht around the head of the sea turtle so that they were on the far side of the island, the bay of Alassio disappearing from view. As they came around the point of the turtle's nose the group could see that they were not alone. A much bigger and more impressive yacht seemed to have dropped anchor as well. Both Ben and Richard teased Simon that his vessel didn't measure up and that they might jump ship to the other one. Simon took their ribbing in good spirit and gave as good as he got, but there was just an edge of distraction as he looked over to the yacht now and again.

Once they had dropped anchor the three got ready to dive, and in no time at all they were enjoying the warmth of the shallow sea. The visibility was crystal clear and they dropped to the rocks on the seabed examining nooks and crannies for fish and various marine invertebrates. Ben had a camera and Simon had furnished Richard with a series of plasticized identification cards held together in one corner with a metal rivet so each card could be opened out. Between them the lads set about photographing and identifying as much of the marine life as they could find. Simon kept a slight distance directing them to things and overseeing that they were doing okay. So engrossed in their task, the boys didn't notice that he also kept looking over to where the other yacht was moored; the pale ghostly shape of its hull just about visible in the distance.

After nearly an hour of diving Simon indicated that they should surface. As they dragged their tanks onto the deck Richard moaned that he wanted to strap on another tank and get back down there. Simon felt a little surge of pride as he heard Ben remind Richard that after almost an hour underwater they needed to have some surface interval time before another dive. While the boys were busy stacking the tanks and flippers Simon went below deck to prepare some food. Ben looked up at the sound of an engine getting nearer and looked over to the big yacht. A small black and red RIB with three men sitting in it was quickly heading their way, its motor throwing up a spume of surf at the back.

'What do you think they want?' asked Richard, shielding his eyes from the sun as he looked in the direction of the noise.

'I dunno but I better go and get Uncle Simon.' Ben disappeared below deck and returned almost immediately, his uncle in tow.

The RIB slowed and pulled up to the small landing stage at the back of the yacht. The three men were all dressed in black, looking almost military rather than holidaymakers. Two of them got out and, abandoning polite protocol, stepped aboard without waiting to be invited. Simon side stepped Ben and put himself in front of the two teenagers.

'What are you doing here?' the leader asked in perfect, although heavily accented English, expressing every syllable clearly as Italians are often want to do when speaking English.

Simon smiled and looked relaxed, although Ben could tell there was an edge of anxiety to him. He replied back with something in Italian. Whatever it was the leader spoke again in English.

'You do realise that this island and its surrounding waters are protected and it is illegal to moor here and dive without the proper permits and permissions.'

'Yes I do and we have all the paperwork in order. I'm rather intrigued as to why you feel the need to come over here and check up on me. That's a private yacht isn't it?' Simon nodded over to the bigger vessel where he could just make out two figures on the deck looking over to them. Their arms raised and elbows sticking out as they watched the proceedings through binoculars.

'It is, but as a private citizen who very much values the need to protect the coastline and all it has to offer, my employer has asked me to come and inform you that you need to move away from here.'

'But as I have just said to you we have all the correct paperwork and permissions to set anchor and dive here.'

The Italian stared at Simon. The tautness of his muscular bulk said that he didn't appreciate anyone messing about with him. His second in command stood just behind him, eyes flicking between Simon and the boys, watching their every move.

'May I see?' the leader of the three held out his hand, his face set.

Simon didn't move but held the man's eyes unwaveringly. 'I'll go and get them for you Uncle Simon, which papers are they?' said Ben, suddenly unable to stand the tension any longer.

'Stay where you are Ben.' Simon instructed, his voice and tone even, but with a steely commanding undertone, eyes still not leaving the man stood in front of him.

'Very well then, if that's how you want it. We have the name and number of your vessel and I am instructed to tell you that we will be reporting you to the relevant official bodies as mooring and diving here illegally.'

'Please do, but I can assure you that it is your employer who will be wasting official time. I'll be very happy to present the documentation to anyone acting in an official capacity that needs to see it.'

The man turned and spoke to the one behind him in Italian. Without another word they got back into the RIB. Simon and the two boys watched as it sped back to the host vessel. Five minutes later there was a flurry of activity on deck and the larger yacht's engines burst into life with a roar. Within a few minutes the vessel was a small white dot as it rounded the coastal promontory and disappeared towards Albenga leaving nothing but a trail of white foam on the surface of the sea.

'What was their problem?' Ben asked, concern written on both boys' faces.

'Well like he said perhaps his employer was just a concerned individual. Or more likely with the sort of money he must have he expected to have the luxury of this side of the island all to himself. Don't worry, if the *Polizia di Stato* or *Carabinieri* come knocking we actually do have all the paperwork in order.'

'Do we? When you told me to stand still and not get the papers I suddenly thought we were here illegally and you were just blagging it.'

'I reckon they were waiting to do some drug deal.' Richard said, his eyes lighting up at the excitement.

'Or an arms deal!' Ben added turning to his new friend, his eyes wide.

'Perhaps there's a stash of something on the island. Maybe they're gun runners and there's an artillery store somewhere in a hidden cave.'

'I know,' said Ben pausing for dramatic effect, 'maybe they're people trafficking.'

Simon laughed at the boys' excitement and ideas as they batted from one to the other. It was when they chorused that they wanted to land on the island and explore it that he said an emphatic 'No'. Before he disappeared below deck to finish getting lunch ready Simon threw a brown coloured bottle to Ben. 'Here, make sure you both put plenty of that on!' Ben looked down at the bottle of sunblock factor 50. Descending the steps to the galley Simon smiled to himself as he heard the boys putting flesh on their more and more outlandish theories while he pulled the ingredients of their tuna salad together.

They spent the afternoon lounging on deck soaking up the warmth of the sun, reading and diving off the yacht into the welcoming blue sea when they needed to cool down. Simon had some coloured plastic rings and they invented games to see who could dive out the furthest to reach them or who could swim round the yacht in the fastest time collecting them up and returning them to the boat. The encounter with the men in black, or any worry that some officials would appear over the horizon, was soon forgotten.

Richard accompanied Ben and Simon on the yacht for the next two days and they explored more reefs around different parts of the island. The large yacht and its threatening men didn't appear again much to Ben's relief. On the third day Mr. and Mrs. Osborne insisted that they took Ben on a trip as a way of saying 'Thank you' and also to give Simon some free time on his own, since they felt he must need it having entertained both boys for so many days. Neither of the boys particularly wanted to go with them. The sedate pace of what they might offer could never measure up to diving trips on their own yacht. So before they made the mood turn sour by pulling faces Simon offered a compromise. He'd take the boys out in the morning, but bring them back at lunchtime at which time the Osbornes could take over. He added quickly that he had some work that he really needed to do in the afternoon and that if they returned Ben at around 6pm he should have finished by then and they could all go out for dinner.

Ben knew better than to raise any objections. His uncle was right and if Simon needed to get on with some work then Ben should just go with the flow and not behave like a spoilt brat. It was only the afternoon and they would be out on the yacht again on Friday anyway.

The plan decided, Mr. and Mrs. Osborne proposed an afternoon trip by train to Monte Carlo. 'Great,' said Ben, trying to drown out Richard's groan. He cast a mischievous glance at his uncle, and rubbing his hands together trying to sound enthusiastic said 'Casino here we come!'

Simon had to suppress a smile at Mrs. Osborne's barely held in whimper of despair.

Chapter 8

The trip to Monte Carlo wasn't as bad as Ben expected it to be. Richard's dad had quite a dry sense of humour and although she got a lot of gentle teasing about her anxieties, Richard's mother took it all in her stride and was able to laugh at herself. They had explored the Natural History Museum and the state apartments in the palace where they had an exhibition on Grace Kelly. The boys had never heard of her, but Mrs. Osborne seemed to wax lyrical about her films. The cathedral was a must so that Mrs. Osborne could see where the actress turned princess was buried. They even had their photo taken on the steps of the casino, but although Mr. Osborne had sided with the boys, his wife had put her foot down at the suggestion of going in and having a flutter.

While they explored Monte Carlo Richard explained that when the new term started he was going to a different school for his A levels. His time at the previous one had been a trial due to the bullying. He hadn't dared tell his parents the half of what he went through, mostly because he was labelled as different. The only son of older parents, not really into football, rugby or cricket, not a follower of the latest music trends. He'd become more quiet and reserved, worrying his mother no end that something was wrong with him. He was predicted to ace his GCSEs and as his current school didn't have such a good academic record he'd managed to persuade his parents to enroll him in a sixth form college. He wanted to be the first person in the family to go to university.

Ben listened in earnest. He liked Richard and although they hadn't known each other long they just sort of fitted together in many ways; although he could see why Richard could be an easy target for bullies. His naïve enthusiasm for things could be so easily and wonderfully crushed by a few mocking comments. It was almost as if without realising it Richard bated you to have a go at him.

In return Ben told Richard about why he was in Alassio with his uncle and that he didn't really want to be going back to the UK, never mind to school and A levels.

Although in walking distance, the Osborne's treated their selves to a taxi from the station to Simon's villa and during the trip it was decided that Richard would stay for dinner. As the taxi pulled away Mrs. Osborne turned to her husband with a satisfied smile, expressing how pleased she was that her son had found what might turn out to be a good friend at last.

'Oh man you've got the new Xbox One X.' Richard rushed up to the sleek black box that sat next to the television and stroked it reverently. 'And a PS4!' He turned to Ben with his mouth wide open.

Ben laughed. 'They're not mine. I'm not sure what my uncle's doing with them either.'

'What have you been playing?'

'Nothing so far. There's been so much other stuff to do. We can have a go at something later if you want.'

'Definitely! I've wanted to play the Xbox One X for ages. My 360's getting past it and while it's still working I won't get a replacement. What games has your uncle got?'

'Dunno. I'm not sure where he keeps them.' Ben walked over to one of the two sideboards in the sitting room and looked through the draws. In the second sideboard he found a range of games for both consoles all stacked in alphabetical order, all first person shoot 'em up style games. Richard was like a small child looking through them and decided on the latest *Call of Duty*.

While Richard set it up Ben went into the kitchen and was relieved when he found that Camilla had left some of her homemade lemonade in the fridge. He'd never tasted anything like it, so sharp but with background sweetness and just what you wanted when it was still thirty degrees and no breeze.

The boys were soon in competition mode and pretty equally matched. They were so engrossed that they hadn't noticed the dusk coming down. The jug of lemonade was long gone and the pile of biscuit and crisp wrappers on the coffee table had finally given way to gravity and tumbled onto the wooden floor when Ben realised the time.

'Blimey it's 9.15' said Ben.

'What?' mumbled Richard as he worked the controls, his fingers a blur over the buttons and his tongue sticking out at the side. 'Noooooo!' he cried as the armoured jeep his character was driving was hit by a missile and erupted into flames. Ben caught his breath as the image gave him a momentary flashback to his parents in his dad's office. Richard dropped the control into his lap and rubbed his eyes. 'What did you say?'

'I said that it was quarter past nine.' With the noise of warfare silenced, the boys could clearly hear the evening song of an army of cicadas buzzing through the trees.

Richard looked at his watch surprised that the hours had slid by so quickly. 'We need to get something proper to eat and then I need to go.' He checked his mobile phone amazed that he had not had any texts or missed calls from his mother, but he knew if he pushed it further it wouldn't be long before she got on a roll.

'Come on,' said Ben getting up and turning some lights on. He walked into the kitchen with Richard following and hunted around to see what Camilla had left for them in the fridge. It didn't take too long to slice the homemade quiche and throw some salad together. The boys ate hungrily at the breakfast bar.

'What time did your uncle say he was coming back?'

'He didn't exactly. He just said he'd see me when I was back from being out with you guys. I thought he'd be here when we arrived.'

Richard pulled a face that sort of tied in with the nagging thought at the back of Ben's mind, that something might not be quite right. His uncle was notoriously private about some things and definitely 'paddled his own canoe' as he'd heard his dad mention many times. But now he was Ben's guardian he would take his responsibility seriously and not leave Ben in the lurch.

'He's probably just delayed. He said he had work to do and it might not have been in Alassio. Perhaps he's had to travel somewhere and got held up?' Richard didn't sound like he was convincing himself never mind his friend. Ben pulled his phone from his pocket and checked it for the nth time since they had stopped playing *Call of Duty*. Still nothing.

'Yeah I'm sure you're right and there's loads of places around here with no signal.'

'I better get off,' said Richard pushing his plate away from him, unsuccessfully stifling a burp at the same time. As he stood his phone beeped. 'Right on cue.' He held the screen in front of Ben. '*Where are you? Love Mum x*'

'I'll walk down the hill with you?' Ben wanted to stretch his legs. As the boys wandered down towards the town following the sharp bends they chatted about tomorrow. Ben said he would meet Richard at the marina at ten o'clock and he'd see if he could convince his uncle to take them further out so they could maybe try diving in deeper water.

It didn't take them long to reach the *sottopassagio* under the railway line. They said their goodbyes and then Ben turned to make his way back up to the villa. As he ambled along he sent a text to his uncle, '*Hope all's okay. When do you think you might be back?'* He stopped and watched the screen, but the little 'Delivered' sign didn't flag up. Strange that his uncle's phone should be off.

Although the temperature had cooled down Ben's shirt was sticking to his back by the time he cleared the last bend before the villa. He was lost in thought and the hypnotic song of the cicadas when suddenly beams of harsh light blinded him. He shielded his eyes as an engine started up and he just had time to jump to the side as a large black 4x4 of some sort revved its engine and sped past. For a brief moment he caught sight of the passenger on his side and was sure it was the lead guy from the expensive yacht. He retrieved his right flip-flop from the road and swore as the strap came away in his hand. Walking barefoot to the electric gates, he pushed the button on his key fob and wondered what the 4x4 was doing. It must have been parked up on the road, since the only sound Ben was aware of was the cicadas' rhythmic buzz, until the vehicle started its engine.

When he got in Ben wandered around the villa and made sure that all the doors were locked and the ground floor windows were closed. He checked his phone and even though the first message still didn't seem to be delivered he sent a second message just in case.

It took Ben a long time to get to sleep, every sound seemed magnified and he couldn't stop his brain from wondering where his uncle was…and what he would do if he still wasn't there in the morning.

Chapter 9

A combination of beeping and buzzing woke Ben from a half sleep. He snatched his phone up from the bedside table and checked the message. *Where are you? R.* Ben checked the time 10.15! He flicked through his messages and checked the one's he had sent to his uncle. Still registering as undelivered. He fired a reply to Richard; *Sorry over slept will be down a.s.a.p.*

All vestiges of tiredness left him as he threw back the thin sheet and headed for the balcony. Peering over the top he looked down into the pool. All the overnight debris was gone and then he spotted Franco's head over the far side of the garden. He walked over to the door and opened it slightly. He could hear Camilla singing to herself as she clattered around in the kitchen. Looking across the landing Simon's bedroom door was still closed. Fending off the urge to knock on it he closed his door and headed to the en suite shower.

'*Ciao!* Well you finally wake up!' Camilla beamed at Ben. 'Sit, I got you big *macedonia* for breakfast.' She placed one of her, by now, famous fruit salads on the breakfast bar next to the two bowls she had put out earlier.

'Is my uncle up yet?' Ben half sat on one of the stools.

'No he not get up also yet.' Camilla emphasised every syllable in her heavily accented English.

'Is he home?'

Camilla frowned slightly at Ben's question and also his bluntness. '*Che cosa?*'

'My uncle. Did he come home last night? I haven't heard from him. No texts.' He held up his phone as if that would make everything crystal clear to Camilla.

'No I no see Signor Simon this morning. He still sleeping.'

Ben slipped off the stool and left the confused housekeeper looking after him as he strode to the staircase. In just a few strides he was outside his uncle's bedroom door.

He knocked gently, 'Uncle Simon?' He didn't want to sound too urgent just in case his uncle opened the door and he had been fussing for nothing. Silence. Ben heard movement behind him and turned. Camilla had followed him upstairs, her expression now one of confusion mixed with a tinge of concern. Ben knocked again, firmer this time. 'Uncle Simon are you in there?'

When there was still no reply Ben turned the door handle and pushed the door wide open. The room was empty and the bed hadn't been slept in. He knew the answer beforehand, but just in case Ben walked over to the en suite bathroom and opened the door. The shower cubicle was completely dry so his uncle hadn't gone off early somewhere.

He clicked on his phone and dialed his uncle's mobile. Nothing. It didn't even go to voicemail.

'My uncle hasn't been home at all since yesterday. We need to find out if he is okay? This isn't like him and he isn't answering his phone.'

Camilla asked Ben to repeat but slower. 'Oh he do this before. He go away for some days then he come back, all okay. It is his work. Come, come and get something to eat.' She gestured back to the bedroom door.

'That might be when he is here on his own, but he wouldn't go away when I am here. Not without saying anything anyway.' Camilla shrugged, her hands palm upwards.

'Please come with me.' Ben pushed past Camilla and went to find Franco. Using Camilla to translate as best as possible and Franco's pigeon Italian they managed to establish that Franco hadn't seen Simon either but that he went out yesterday afternoon in the Audi TT and it was still missing from the garage.

Ben's phone beeped again. *'What's happening? Are we diving today or what? R.'*

Ben grunted his frustration as Camilla and Franco talked and he tapped rapidly on his phone. *Problem. No diving today. Can't find Uncle Simon. Didn't come home yesterday. Sorry*.

Ben suddenly remembered the black 4x4 that must have been sitting outside the house last night. He grabbed Camilla by the arm, 'We need to call the police. I think something has happened to him. The police! *Polizia*' He added for good measure seeing the confusion on Camilla's face.

'No, no. We wait. I tell to you Signor Simon he go to work like this before then he come back. Please Ben there is no need to get upset. You'll see. Now come in the house and get some breakfast.'

Ben felt torn; he didn't know what to do. He was sure something must have happened to his uncle, but at the same time Camilla knew his uncle's movements here and he didn't. He still couldn't get over the fact that his uncle wouldn't just take off overnight with Ben being here though. His phone buzzed again. *Cleared it with mum and dad. I'm coming up to you. I'll be there in about twenty minutes.*

Although he wasn't sure what the added presence of Richard would bring to the situation, Ben felt a degree of relief that he would have someone to talk to in English. Ben looked up from his phone, Franco had disappeared back to work and he watched the receding form of Camilla for a second before following her back to the kitchen.

'What's happened?' Richard asked breathlessly after hurrying up the long climb from the sea front. Ben looked past Richard. 'It's all right, mum and dad have decided to walk into Laigueglia. I told them your uncle's work had over run and you'd invited me up to the pool.'

Ben looked over at Camilla who was cleaning with one ear open. He wasn't sure exactly how much English she understood so he took Richard up to his bedroom.

'You know my uncle went out working on something yesterday afternoon.'

'Yeah of course, I was here.'

'I've sent him two texts and tried to ring him several times. His phone is switched off; it's dead. He never does that. He didn't come home last night and the car's missing. Camilla says he takes off with work like this now and again and I shouldn't worry, but I know he wouldn't do something like this without saying anything because I'm here. Oh, and last night after walking you down the hill, I was just getting round the last bend before the gates and I was almost mown down by a massive 4x4 that I think was parked in the road.

Like it was waiting outside the house.' Richard's eyes opened wide and he was about to say something but Ben cut across him. 'And I think that guy who threatened us from the posh boat was in the passenger seat.'

Richard let out a long breath. 'You think your uncle going off might have something to do with them then?'

'I'm not sure, but I don't like it. I wanted to call the police but Camilla said not to. How long do you think I should wait?'

'Well if you get onto them too soon and she tells them it's part of his normal pattern they aren't going to take anything seriously. Maybe you had better wait a bit longer.'

Ben gave in reluctantly, but the unease that was gnawing at his stomach didn't calm down. Throughout the rest of the day he kept checking his phone, he tried to text and leave a message several times but got the same result. Richard, for his part, tried to keep the conversation buoyant and on varied subjects, but their conversation kept coming back to the yacht, the heavies and where was Simon Weir?

The public beach by the round tower was packed, but they managed to squeeze their towels on a small area of sand, much to the annoyance of some German tourists who were trying to spread out beyond their need. Richard challenged Ben to a swim as far as the line of buoys they could just make out bobbing up and down, which marked the boundary for speedboats.

By mid afternoon Ben couldn't stand it any longer, he needed to do something active rather than passively waiting for his uncle to get in touch. The boys decamped from the beach to the small outdoor café in the Piazzetta Fraticappuccini.

'So what do you suggest we do?' Richard asked before he took a huge bite out of his Siciliana panino.

'We can search the Internet and see if we can find anything out about the yacht.'

'Did you get its name or a number?' Richard asked already suspecting the answer. Ben shook his head. 'I don't think you'll get very far with that one then.'

'Maybe there's something back at the villa, something to go on at least?'

'That'll mean going through your uncle's things.'

'Yeah I suppose so.' Ben's heart sank at the thought of betraying Simon's trust rifling through his private things, but what other option did they have. He was convinced that Simon wouldn't just suddenly turn up. It was now twenty-four hours since there had been any sort of contact.

'You can look at his computer?' Richard said nonchalantly as if he accessed people's private computers as a matter of course.

Ben pulled a face at the thought of that. 'It's probably all password protected anyway.'

After a few minutes of silence Ben looked at his watch, 'They should have left by now. Come on before I change my mind.' He took his wallet from his back pocket and went over to the kiosk to pay for their lunch.

The first thing Ben did when they got back to the villa was to check the garage. Still no Audi. Everything was locked up and the shutters fastened to keep the villa cool, but even so Ben called out Franco and Camilla's names just in case. When there was no reply he suggested that they start with Simon's bedroom.

The boys entered quietly and spoke in whispers as if expecting to be caught red handed at any moment. The room was tidy, everything in its place and ordered. Simon's clothes were all neatly folded and organized in drawers and the wardrobe.

'You're uncle a bit OCD?' asked Richard as he pulled open a sock draw looking down at the pairs all neatly folded into each other and arranged in rows.

'I think he's just organized,' said Ben giving his uncle the benefit of the doubt.

Once Ben had got over the initial reluctance of going through his uncle's personal things he got into the swing of it, but making sure to put everything back in its original position. Richard on the other hand seemed to be loving the experience, it was as if he was on some sort of spying exercise, which made his disappointment at finding nothing interesting all the more intense than Ben's.

Half way through the exercise Richard had sat back on his haunches. 'What exactly are we looking for?'

'I don't know? Anything that seems odd, anything that relates to that yacht or the island. I'm sure we'll know it when we find it. If we find it.'

'Okay so we're just looking for anything basically?'

'I guess so.'

'Glad we cleared that one up then!' Richard said, one eyebrow raised. An hour later the boys had been through everything, even looking under the bed. Richard lifting the foot end while Ben scrabbled about on his hands and knees. Nothing.

'Where now?' asked Richard as Ben closed the bedroom door behind him.

Ben looked across the landing to the study door. 'In there but I don't know how we'll get in. It's locked and I've never seen the windows to that room open, besides it doesn't have a balcony.'

Richard walked over to the door and rattled the handle as if needing to prove to himself that Ben was telling the truth. 'There's got to be a spare key of some sort. Are there any extra keys on the ring your uncle gave you?'

Ben ran downstairs and returned with his house keys. 'A couple but I'm not sure they'd fit that sort of lock.' He handed them to Richard who tried them, but they were far too small.

'There's got to be a spare somewhere. If he's got important stuff in there he won't just have the one key surely.'

The boys started downstairs, working their way from drawer to drawer and room to room systematically. A junk drawer in the kitchen turned up a handful of loose keys but none of them fit the study lock. Their spirits dampening they started upstairs.

'Ta dah!' Richard sang, as he emerged beaming from one of a pair of store cupboards on the landing holding up a small brass door key.

'Where was it?'

'Taped to the underside of a shelf at the back. I had to feel for it.' Richard held the key out to Ben. 'This has got to be it.'

Ben took the key eagerly, and inserting it into the lock, turned it with a rewarding click as the mechanism responded and the door opened. He smiled at Richard, 'Bingo!'

Chapter 10

The room was smaller than Ben was expecting, but as per Simon's style everything was neatly arranged and tidy. The red light on the computer console showed it was in standby mode, the same on the wireless printer that sat on a small table against one wall.

'Let's try drawers and things before we tackle the computer,' Ben said to Richard. Almost unspoken they worked out a method of approach between them, dividing the room by half and then systematically moving from one drawer, bookshelf or cupboard to the next. They found papers in Italian, folders of accounts pertaining to the villa, what looked like expense sheets for the running of the villa, receipts for purchases, petrol receipts for the car. The study seemed to hold everything and anything that they didn't want to find, but nothing that might give them a clue as to where Simon could be.

'I guess it's the computer now then,' Richard rubbed his hands together.

'I dunno, it just feels like we're going too far.'

'Well we've been through all his personal stuff in his bedroom and broken into his study so I don't think having a look at this computer is going to make things any worse.'

'Technically we haven't broken in,' said Ben defensively trying to justify things to himself as much as anything else. Richard didn't say anything but just stood there with an expression that screamed 'yeah right'.

'Up to you?' Richard shrugged.

Ben took a deep breath and sat in the leather chair facing the monitor. He pushed the start button as Richard moved to stand at the side of him. As the screen came to life it was the anticlimax he had half expected, the computer was asking him for a password.

He started to type in as many things as he could think of – Simon's initials and year of birth, then reversing it. He thought up the names of places Simon had mentioned, where he was born or had been to including Alassio. All of them failed.

'This is useless!' he spat out, a mixture of frustration and despair.

'Get up!' Richard ordered tugging at Ben's t-shirt.

'What makes you think you can do any better?'

'This is an iMac and it doesn't look like anything fancy has been done to it, just straightforward password protection. I might be able to get into it.'

'What, so you're an expert hacker now are you?'

'No,' Richard said firmly, starting to get a bit fed up with Ben, 'but I do know a thing or two about computers. We do have them at Academies you know, it's not just private schools!'

Ben tried not to look too sheepish as he slid out of the chair letting Richard sit down.

'Looks like there is only one user registered, which will be your uncle. I might be able to bypass and reset the password to something we make up. The downside will be that I can't then reset it with the original password, so your uncle will definitely know we have been on it…well, that someone has hacked it anyway.'

Ben shrugged his shoulders. 'I guess we've got to do it. We can deal with the explanations later.'

Richard made a show of linking his fingers and stretching out his arms as if he were about to play a piano concerto.

He held down the start key turning the computer off and while it was rebooting hit the command S key. 'If I'm going to reset the administrator password I need to gain root access.'

Ben watched amazed as the screen went black and a long list of white commands and scripted pathways scrolled downwards. Once it had finished Richard scrolled down to the end where there were a series of 'root' commands. Alongside one of them he typed in a coded instruction. This process went on for a little while, Richard typing in coded instructions and hitting enter, until he arrived at a command that allowed him to type in a new password.

'OK what shall we have?' He looked at Ben expectantly.

Ben thought for a second and took his parents initials along with some numbers for rearranged dates of birth. As he spoke Richard's fingers hovered over the keyboard tapping in the information. At the end he tapped the return key. The computer seemed to accept the password change and then the information on the screen came to a stand still.

'What now?' Ben asked, a sense of panic that something had gone wrong creeping into his voice.

'Now, we need to reboot it.' Richard typed in the commands and the computer screen went blank. Both boys lent towards the screen in silent expectation. After a few seconds the screen came to life and asked them for the password. Richard entered the information and looked at Ben as his finger hovered over the enter key. 'Keep your fingers crossed this works.' He brought his finger down and pushed the key.

'We're in!' he shouted a second later. 'Oh yes, am I good or what?'

'Yeah you didn't do too badly.' Ben smiled at Richard knowing that there was no way he could have achieved the same result.

'Now let's see what we have here.' Richard clicked on the 'Finder' icon and started to scroll through the information. After going through the document folders the boys tried to search the Internet browsing history, but Simon had clearly deleted that after he had last used the computer.

'I can't believe we have wasted all that time for nothing.' Richard sat back in the chair defeated. Ben rubbed his eyes.

'I thought there'd be something there. Nothing about Simon's work. Not even a single document about Gallinara or the yacht.'

In fact both boys had been surprised at how little information there was stored on the computer's hard drive. They had tried a couple of memory sticks from the desk drawer but again there was little of interest. Simon had obviously had some great holidays by the photos they were pulling up from all around the world. Apart from a handful of selfies though, none of the photographs showed anybody else. They were all of sights, events, scenes or buildings. The only time both boys had watched in silence was when they opened up a folder simply titled 'Family'. Ben's smiling parents came into view in a group shot outside Luxborough

House. It was taken some years ago and Ben stood in front of everybody as a toddler, fat legs sticking out of short dungarees as he pointed at a blurred vision of a dog that was running across the posed shot.

Ben answered Richard's questions about the photos and family members until he couldn't bear to see anymore. He ejected the memory stick and pocketed it.

Ben wandered over to the door. 'Let's get something to eat and rethink this. There's got to be something here that's of use. Why would Uncle Simon go to the lengths he has to keep this room locked and the key hidden if there wasn't anything of any importance?'

Richard pushed the chair back from the desk and looked at his watch, 'Well we've probably got time to go through things again if you feel up to it. Maybe we just missed something.'

After the boys had eaten they decided to start from the upper floor of the villa and work their way down this time. Ben suggested they start with the study. All feelings of embarrassment about going through his uncle's were things forgotten by the frustration of their lack of results.

Richard started pulling open drawers, but Ben stood by the window looking out and then he turned to face the room. His eyes narrowed. Something wasn't right but he couldn't put his finger on it.

'Hey I'm not doing this all on my own you know?' Richard moaned as he put a pile of folders back in a drawer and opened the one below it.

Ben called him over to where he stood. 'There's something not quite right about the dimensions of this room. It should be bigger than it is.' Richard pulled a face as if to say 'what are you taking about?'

'Look,' said Ben feeling the need to explain further. 'Here's the end wall of the building, here's the window and the window to next door is much further away than it should be if the wall is there.' Ben pointed at the wall between the study and the bedroom next door. Richard still looked blank. 'The windows should be equidistant from this dividing wall so that everything looks even outside, but it isn't, this wall is too far this way.'

Ben ignored Richard's look of confusion and marched to the large bedroom next door. He looked at a flat wall. Walking up to it he tapped along it, the sound was dull. He walked into the wide landing area to where one of the landing cupboards looked back at him. He then walked back into the study. 'I'm sure this wall is too far this way.' He tapped the wall and it made a hollow sound, quite different to the bedroom wall.

'Oh I see,' Richard's face lit up, as he finally understood what Ben was getting at. 'You think this is a false wall? Yes, I can see why you'd think that now.' Both boys walked along the wall tapping it at various heights. It sounded hollow from skirting board to ceiling all the way along.

'I've got an idea.' Richard rushed out onto the landing, Ben close on his heels. He flung open the landing cupboard door. 'Here take these,' Richard handed Ben some coats on their hangers; he then pulled out a vacuum cleaner and a dustpan and brush. Ben took them all and stacked them neatly behind him. Once the cupboard was emptied Richard stepped into the shallow space and tapped the back wall. The boys were rewarded with yet more hollow sounds.

Richard turned to Ben, his eyes wide. 'There's a space between the two rooms, roughly the width of this cupboard.'

'So how do we get in without knocking the wall down?'

The back wall was made of six wooden panels. 'I'll take this side and you take that side,' Richard said to Ben, squashing over so his friend could squeeze in next to him. They started to run their fingers along the edges of the panels, pushing them now and again to see if they moved. Ben stood on his tiptoes and reached up to the top line of wooden beading. He slid his fingers along it until he felt a small bump. It felt cold, like metal, rather than the warmer wood.

'I think I've found something!' Richard stood back so Ben could stand square in front of the panelling. He pushed the button down and there was a light click, one half of the panelling swung inwards. As Ben looked into the gloom he could see a narrow space and in the darkness small lights of various colours blinked on and off.

Ben squeezed his way through the panel doorway and ran his hands along the walls on either side until he located a switch. Three spotlights in the ceiling came on casting a soft yellow glow. As Ben stepped further into the room the temperature rose several degrees and the air was stuffy.

'Wow,' Richard said, his voice expressing the wonderment Ben felt at what lay in front of them.

One wall was full of computer screens; several of them cast a greenish glow, as they seemed to be streaming through data of their own volition. Presumably Simon had set them on a task and they were working their way through it. A large metal cupboard was at the end of the small room, its back against the outside wall, above it the boys could see a narrow grill that led along the top of the wall to the outside; just under the eaves of the roof so it would be hard to see from the outside. A counter top under the computers serving as a narrow desk was littered with papers and hand written notes.

'Looks like we've found what we were looking for.' Ben said, his eyes wide as he continued to scan around the room.

Richard rubbed his hands together excitedly, 'You start that end of the desk and I'll start down here.'

'Look!' Ben passed a photograph to Richard.

'That's definitely him.' Richard confirmed as he looked at the grainy black and white shot of the Italian who had boarded the boat. It looked like it had been taken from a distance with the camera on maximum magnification. 'Why do you think your uncle has been spying on him?'

'Hopefully we'll find out, look there are more.' Ben moved down to where Richard stood and laid out several photographs that looked like they could have been taken at the same time. Most were of an older man, smartly dressed with a shock of white hair.

'You know him?' asked Richard. Ben shook his head. He gathered the photos together and put them on one side.

They worked consistently for about an hour and then came out of the room to get some fresh air and discuss their findings.

Simon seemed to have been investigating a company called VM Laboratories and its founder, a scientist called Dr Henrik von Moltke. The boys had found a printout of a LinkedIn profile showing a photograph of von Moltke. He was the white haired guy in the blown up photos.

'So I wonder why this von Moltke has caught uncle Simon's interest?'

'I don't know,' said Richard, 'but I found this, seems like your trip here wasn't all due to your uncle's concern about your wellbeing.'

Richard passed Ben a sheet of paper with information written in Simon's own handwriting. It was a list of von Moltke's travel arrangements with a ring drawn around the dates he would be in Albenga. 'Looks like he's back to the UK very soon,' said Ben.

'Come on, we better see if we can find anything more, we've still got the drawers to go through, and that cupboard at the end.' Ben stood up from where he had been sitting on the landing floor and stretched, papers still clutched in his hand. 'What is it?' a frown gathered across his forehead as he looked down at Richard who hadn't moved.

Richard looked down at Ben's feet, obviously uncomfortable. 'There's erm, something else I found. I, I think you should read it. It looks pretty official.'

Ben sat down heavily opposite Richard; he felt his heart sink in his chest and his blood drop down to his feet. 'Sounds serious,' he said quietly.

Richard reached for some folded papers he had tucked down by his side, almost out of view. He held them out to Ben and then leant back against the wall giving his friend space to assimilate the information.

Ben's fingers shook as he unfolded the papers. The first thing he noticed was the large government crest emblazed at the top. It was an official forensic report on the explosion that had killed his parents. He read slowly and methodically. It was clear from the forensic report that the 'accident' had been nothing of the sort. The report stated that there was a prime explosion in his father's office that set off a series of chain reactions throughout the building. The report concluded that it was a definite act of sabotage, terrorism or murder, but since they could not offer any information on a perpetrator or motive they could not say which.

'Are you okay?'

Ben jumped at the sound of Richard's voice. His friend had been so still that Ben had forgotten his presence. Ben looked up, his face white, his eyes glassy with tears. 'They, they were killed...murdered.' His voice faltered, 'They were murdered, and people knew.' Ben's voice had become stronger and colour flushed up into his face. 'Look, look at the date on this. Weeks ago and nobody has said anything. Why haven't the police been in contact? Why hasn't Uncle Simon said anything to me about it, he clearly knows.' Ben was shouting now, his hands trembling, the tears rolling down his cheeks.

Richard knelt in front of his distraught friend. He didn't really know what to do, and hesitated before he put his hands on Ben's shoulders and tried to steady him. He put his face close to Ben's. 'It's okay Ben.

Take your time.' He rubbed Ben's shoulders awkwardly hoping he was doing some good to console him.

'I think your uncle knew about this and is investigating it himself. Otherwise why would he have all this information? I've no idea why the police aren't onto it. It looks to me like your uncle thinks this von Moltke guy and his company have something to do with it. I reckon all this has something to do with where he is now as well.'

His initial shock and gut reaction calmed, Ben listened in silence to Richard and nodded his head. 'Yeah, yeah I think you're right.' He pulled a tissue from his pocket and rubbed his face. 'We've got to find him!' Ben pushed himself up the wall and took a deep breath. As he stepped back into the secret room he turned to look at Richard, 'Thanks.'

The boys carried on working methodically through the room.

'Where do you reckon this fits?' Ben asked holding up a small silver key he had found taped to the underside of a drawer. They scanned the room looking for something with a lock on it.

'Looks like it's gotta be here,' Richard indicated the handle of the metal cupboard which had a small keyhole. He twisted the handle, which refused to move. 'It's locked. Try the key.' He stood out of the way so that Ben could get to it.

The door opened smoothly and silently. 'Bloody hell!' said Ben quietly as he leant to one side letting Richard see. Richard didn't utter a word but just sucked in air nosily at what the cupboard contained.

Looking back at the boys were a series of guns; rifles, handguns and a shotgun hung from small pins and hooks projecting from the metal walls. At the bottom were several small shelves with boxes of ammunition. Hanging inside the door was a range of evil looking knives, the light bulb's stark glare reflecting off blades of various sizes.

'What do you think that is?' said Richard quietly as if he was afraid speaking normally would give them away to nobody in particular. He pointed over Ben's shoulder to a black piece of equipment hanging from its strap. Ben reached over and removed it.

'Looks like a pair of binoculars.' He put them to his eyes, 'Oh wow! Night vision binoculars.'

'Let me have a go?' Richard held out his hand eagerly. 'Man, it's like Night Ops on *Call of Duty.*'

'I reckon we shouldn't touch any of this stuff,' Ben said.

Richard looked back into the cupboard and nodded his head. 'Except these, these could come in useful.' He clutched the night vision binoculars to his chest.

Ben locked up the cupboard and, apart from the papers and photographs he thought relevant, they left everything as they had found it. It didn't take them long to close the paneling at the back of the cupboard and replace everything they had removed earlier.

'What now?' Richard asked with enthusiasm, his eyes bright with the chase.

'I'm not sure but I'm not sitting around here waiting all night again. Now we've got those how about we see if there's anything happening where we saw the yacht?'

'Cool. I'd better call mum and dad first though. Tell them I'm staying over night with you if that's okay?'

Ben went downstairs to get things ready while Richard called his parents. A few minutes later Richard came to join him in the kitchen. 'That's that sorted. I told them I was keeping you company overnight and that I'd call them in the morning to let them know if your uncle's come back. I had to fend mum off from coming up too, dad's going to distract her. I won't be able to stop her in the morning though so we need to be prepared for her, all guns blazing, if he's not back by then.'

Ben nodded, not really taking in what Richard was saying. He needed to work out some sort of plan of action and needless to say that didn't involve Richard's parents.

Chapter 11

Ben found a key for the black Vespa on a hook in the garage. He shook the moped from side to side and heard the familiar slosh of fuel in its tank.

'You know how to work that thing?' Richard said from the garage doorway looking unconvinced at the idea of riding it.

'Yeah, I've got a grass tracking bike back at home that I race round the orchard on. It can't be too different to riding that.'

'I suppose so,' Richard still didn't sound convinced.

'Here put this on!' Ben threw a helmet over to Richard and then placed a second he'd found over his own head. Kicking back the scooter's stand Ben carefully reversed it out of the garage and aimed it at the gates. 'You got the night vision?'

Richard held up the black case before putting the strap over his neck. Ben got on the scooter and turned the key, the Vespa sprung into life with its high-pitched *pap, pap, pap* as the engine turned over. 'Get on then!'

'How do I hang on?'

'Easiest is to wrap your arms around me. As we go round corners, follow my body and lean into the bend, but not too much or you'll have us over. You'll soon get the hang of it. It's easy.'

'If you say so,' said Richard tentatively, his earlier bravado momentarily deserting him.

Ben opened the gates and set off. He took the sharp bends slowly until he cut under the railway and then sped along the main road. He remembered the road up to Santa Croce from his return walk with Simon during his first few days there. They had packed some lunch and then set off on foot up a long winding path through the backs of Alassio to Solva. Once they'd had a look round the little village and the church they had followed the road out to Santa Croce and then back down into Alassio.

Ben turned left off the main road and passed under the arch following the single-track road. Almost immediately the Vespa started to climb and at a couple of points its engine whined even more, objecting to the weight of the two of them and the gradient of the road. They passed the gardens with the viewpoints out across the bay towards Isola Gallinara and turned into the car park in front of the small chapel of Santa Croce.

Ben killed the engine. The evening was still warm and it was a relief to get their crash helmets off. A single streetlight illuminated the centre of the car park, its beam casting a dim light at the edges of its range. 'We need to follow the path down there,' Ben pointed to a break in the greenery at the side of the chapel. He dug in his pocket and retrieved the small torch he had placed there earlier.

'So what exactly are we looking for?' Richard asked, still a little unsure of their exact mission.

'If we go along the path for about twenty minutes or so we should be able to see the back side of the island where we anchored to dive the reef that first time. We can see if that yacht's there for a start. Like I said, I'm sure the guy in that 4x4 was the lead heavy who came to tell us off.'

'Jeez what was that?' Richard ducked down, his hands over his head as a dark shape suddenly swooped towards him and then disappeared into the gloom as fast as it had appeared.

Ben laughed. 'It was only a bat. The streetlight attracts insects and the bats come to feed on them.'

Richard stood up straight anxiously looking around. 'They won't do you any harm and they definitely won't fly into you. Come on let's get going.' Ben led the way; Richard followed still looking left and right above his head as if readying himself for another bat attack.

The track was rough and the boys had to take it slowly for fear of tripping or going over on an ankle. Ben used the torch in the darkest sections that were overgrown with dense, scrubby trees forming a canopy blocking out any moonlight. As they picked their way along they stopped every now and again where the bush cover cleared and looked out over the sea. Ben used the night vision binoculars. At one point he had a clear view down into the marina, picking out individual boats moored to their posts. Everything in his field of view glowed a spectral green, with lights showing up as intense light green spots. He had to switch his view quickly a few times due to car headlights that suddenly angled round the hairpins in the road to shine their distant headlights directly into the binoculars.

'These are wicked!' said Ben, holding them out so that Richard could have a go.

'Wow! You can see right across the town to the slopes on the far side. Even Laigueglia doesn't look that far away. I can even see the lights on the pier. These are some piece of kit. I've got to get myself a pair when I get back to London.'

'I think these might be out of our price range,' said Ben taking them back.

By the time the boys had got to a point where they could see the far side of Isola Gallinara, they had sweat running down their backs and wished they had the foresight to bring a bottle of water with them.

'Look, let's get up there.' Ben pointed to a large rocky outcrop up the slope, about twenty feet from the path. As they made to sit on the rock, something suddenly burst from the dry vegetation with a loud rustling sound.

'Holy crap!' swore Richard, jumping back up again. 'What was that?' his heart was beating a rapid tattoo so hard if felt like it would leap out of his chest.

'Probably a lizard. Jeez you scared me then.'

'I scared *you*? This place is crawling with risky stuff, plus I'm getting eaten alive by flies and crap.' Richard swatted the side of his neck to add dramatic effect. 'What are you laughing at?'

'I wish I could have seen your face when that lizard darted.'

'Yeah, well if you could see it now it'd be saying something else to you!' Ben laughed even harder and then suddenly remembered what they were there for and shushed himself and Richard before they got any louder and attracted unwanted attention. Although who was in earshot at that time in the middle of nowhere was anybody's guess.

Having settled down on the rock Ben raised the night vision glasses to his eyes, quickly finding the shoreline he looked further out to sea. The greenish mound of the island came into view. Ben adjusted the magnification and focusing until he could see the shape of trees and clearly pick out the outlines of abandoned monastery buildings.

'See anything?' asked Richard impatient for a go.

Ben carried on sweeping along the shoreline of the island and over the sea away from its shore. Then he saw a large pale green shape. 'There it is!'

'What?'

'The yacht.' Ben was sure it was the same one. He could see crewmembers on deck, by the way their green shapes glowed Ben guessed they were all dressed in black. He tried to magnify further and could just make out faces, although the resolution was not as clear at that high magnification. He scanned for the lead guy who came to their yacht but didn't think he could see him.

'Let me look?' Richard held out his hands unable to contain his excitement any further.

Ben handed the binoculars over. 'Find the island first, come down to the shoreline by the little harbour and then scan out to your left.' Richard followed the instructions, barely daring to breathe so that he could keep his hands steady.

'You found it?'

'Yeah, they look busy down there but can't quite see what it is they are doing. They seem to be moving things in crates, stacking them up on the deck. Oh, oh…'

'What?' said Ben urgently.

'Some tall guy in a very smart suit has just come up on board, mass of white hair like some smooth French painter or composer. Hey, watch it!'

Ben had grabbed the binoculars and was pulling them towards his face, not realising Richard had put the strap round his neck. When he had control of the glasses he fixed on the new guy. Richard was right, he wasn't dressed like the others and seemed to be ordering the men about. He stood one hand in his jacket pocket, the other waving a long cigar about. Ben watched as the end glowed an intense spot of green as the man sucked on it at intervals. 'Von Moltke!' Ben said quietly, 'It has to be.'

'My turn again,' said Richard. 'I wish we'd found two pairs of these things in your uncle's secret room.'

Ben passed the binoculars over. 'What do you think those crates might be for? None of that looks like some rich guy just enjoying his boat and the peace and quiet of the back side of Gallinara.'

Richard started to laugh. 'What's so funny?'

'Just thought of this rich guy up a bird's bum?'

'What?'

'You said round the backside of Gallinara. Gallinara, bird. A bird's backside, get it?'

Ben groaned. 'You know there are scorpions as well as lizards in all this undergrowth.' Richard's laugh drained away as he scanned the area where he sat. A few seconds later he ignored Ben's silent snigger as he raised the binoculars.

'Yeah that's definitely von Moltke and they look like some sort of storage crates to me. Presumably they are going to off load them if they are arranging them on the deck, perhaps taking them to the island.' Richard scanned right and took in the greenish glow of Gallinara. 'There's activity in the small harbour. They seem to be bringing some one down from the island and walking them along the breakwater towards a small dinghy.'

'What? Let me look.' Ben said urgently reaching for the glasses again.

'Ben, I…I think it might be your uncle.' Richard said hesitatingly, before he relinquished his grip on the apparatus.

Ben's heart was jumping up into his throat as he put the binoculars to his eyes. He swore in frustration as he frantically tried to alter the magnification to get a clearer, larger view of the island's harbour wall. Once he had pin pointed the activity, he saw three men walking with someone who was clearly a captive, one in front, the prisoner following and two behind. They were walking to the end of the wall where a small inflatable dinghy was waiting, one man already in the boat. Ben held his breath as he scanned the prisoner, whose hands were tied or handcuffed behind his back. It definitely looked like Uncle Simon's build and hairstyle, but the man had his back to Ben all the time. 'Come on, turn around…please.' Ben whispered to himself. 'Whoever it is must have swum to the island.'

Ben could see the man was dressed in a wetsuit, the top half hanging down around his waist like a partially shed skin. He was aware of Richard sitting right next to him, his apprehension palpable over the short distance that separated their bodies.

The lead man got down into the dinghy and it was clear the prisoner was meant to follow. Once the captive man was down he looked around as if assessing where to sit. As he scanned around he looked directly back to the mainland, almost as if he was looking directly at Ben. Uncle Simon! It was definitely him. His face looked marked as if it was dirty…or, they were the darker patches of injury. Ben reckoned his uncle wouldn't have let himself be taken without putting up a fight. 'It is him.' Ben said quickly, as if he didn't want to interrupt what was playing out in front of him.

As Ben watched, the man who had got into the boat shoved Simon as if forcing him to just sit down anywhere. Simon retaliated by spinning to face his aggressor and lurched forward, his forehead connecting with the nose of the other man. As soon as the commotion broke out one of the two men still standing on the wall reached inside his jacket and pullet out what looked like a gun, pointing it at Simon. There was a single second where time seemed to stand still like a freeze frame; the man pointing the gun at Simon, Simon looking up at him, Ben watching them both. Then Ben saw a small but intense green flash, a split second later the boys heard the muffled bang of gunfire echo around the bay. Simon collapsed into the boat.

'No!' shouted Ben, his hands shaking, but he kept the binoculars raised. He had to see what they did next.

'What's happening? What are they doing? That sounded like a gunshot. Ben tell me what you can see.' Richard's questions tumbled out one on the back of the other. He stood up and held his hands over his eyes, squinting, trying to make out what was going on.

Ben watched as the other two men got into the boat. The motor started and it sped off towards the yacht. He watched two of the men haul his uncle up the steps, dumping him before the feet of the man in the suit.

The whole thing had only taken a few minutes but it seemed like hours. Ben set the glasses down in his lap, his mind numb. He tried to speak to Richard, but the words stuck in his throat, he coughed and tried to work his tongue in his dry mouth.

'They…they shot him. He head butted one of the men and they shot him. They took him back to the yacht.'

'Oh jeez Ben, we've got to get back. We've got to go to the police. Now, before they get away.' He pulled his mobile from his pocket. 'What's the Italian for 999?'

'I dunno.' Ben replied absently, as if his voice was on autopilot from his mind.

Richard swore and shoved his phone back into his pocket. He reached down and pulled at Ben's t-shirt, trying to get him to move into action. 'Come on Ben, snap out of it will you. We've got to go.'

As Ben stood slowly, not taking his eyes off the yacht, Richard was already pushing him down towards the path. Ben stopped suddenly causing Richard to knock into him, 'Wait! Look.'

Richard followed Ben's finger looking further out to sea. He could just make out the white foam of churned sea and hear the distant rumble of a deep engine as a solid black shape moved towards it. Ben looked through the night vision binoculars again. A second vessel larger than the yacht, was heading to their meeting point; its bigger engine eating up the distance between them quickly. Ben watched as the vessel slowed and pulled up alongside the yacht. Ropes were thrown between them to anchor them together while the crates were moved from one deck to the other. There was no sign of Uncle Simon. The transfer of the crates complete, both vessels sped in opposite directions. The bigger one back out to sea and the luxury yacht back around the point towards Albenga.

'Let's get going,' Ben said urgently as they hurried back to the Vespa.

Chapter 12

Ben opened up the throttle on the moped and it sped down the winding road. Richard tucked his head in behind Ben's back and held on for dear life, trying to remember to lean into the bends as Ben took them at break neck speed. The Vespa shot under the railway arch and burst forth onto the main road. Ben hadn't even slowed at the junction and sent up a silent prayer to his parents that nothing was coming in either direction. It took no time at all before he was pulling up in front of the *Commissariato di Alassio* on the Viale D. Hanbury. He had remembered its location from a conversation he'd had with his uncle about the difference between the *Polizia* and the *Carabinieri*.

'You reckon there'll be anyone there at this time?'

Ben looked at his watch, astonished to see it was almost a quarter to midnight. 'Of course there will, it's a police station.'

Ben raced up to the door and turned the handle, but the door wouldn't budge. 'What? Who locks the police station door?' He started to bang on the door, shouting and making as much noise as possible. Richard joined in and after a few minutes they heard a gruff voice loudly shouting '*Basta! Basta!*' Rapid, hard booted steps echoed across a marble floor, followed by the scrape of metal as bolts were drawn back and the door swung open revealing a well lit marble concourse and a large, angry looking Italian policeman, his eyes hard and his lips taught.

'*Cosa vuoi?*' he barked.

'Help, we need help.' Ben shouted. When he got no reaction he pointed to himself and Richard. 'English. Err...*Ingelese, non italiano.*' He just hoped he could get some information across. 'You speak English?'

The policeman spoke to them in Italian, gesticulating wildly as if that might help them to understand. Ben pushed his way in followed by Richard. 'Does anybody speak English? We need help. *Aiuto!*' Ben pointed his fingers like a gun and said 'Bang, Bang. *Aiuto! Inglese!*'

The policeman muttered something in Italian that neither boy understood but hoped it was something positive. He pointed at a row of chairs and said in labored English 'You sit there now.' Ben was about to open his mouth but the policeman held up his hand to silence him and then turned on his heel marching quickly away and up a flight of marble stairs to the floor above.

'What's all this "bang, bang?"' Richard said holding his fingers up to make a gun. He laughed teasing Ben to try and lighten the atmosphere.

'Well what was I supposed to? It got his attention didn't it? Besides I didn't hear you trying to flex your Italian vocabulary too strongly.'

'Fair enough,' said Richard shrugging his shoulders. 'So I guess we sit here and wait to see what happens next.'

The boys had been sitting there for about fifteen minutes and were debating whether or not they should go and look for someone when they heard a door close, followed by voices and footsteps that were getting louder. Two men in uniform came down the stairs towards them, one was the policeman that let them in, and the other a younger man who had an air of authority and who the older policeman seemed to defer to.

The younger man came towards them. He extended his hand along with a quick smile and a nod of the head. 'Gentlemen. I understand you need to speak with someone. Something about a gun I think?' His English was pretty good and seeing his chance Ben rushed into trying to explain what had happened.

'Please, please,' said the officer holding up both hands. 'Come with me and we can sit down and discuss this properly.' Without waiting he turned and walked back up the marble staircase. Ben and Richard followed behind.

'I am Giancarlo Offredi and I am in charge here this night. Now what is it that you want to tell to me?' Offredi sat behind the large heavy oak desk and indicated the two seats on the other side. He sat back, one hand on the desk and the other stroking his chin as he watched the boys.

Ben looked at Richard, drawing strength from his friend's nod and smile of encouragement. He took a deep breath and then started from the beginning when he and the Osbornes had come back from Monte Carlo to find Simon absent from the villa and that he had not been seen since. He told the officer about his attempts to contact his uncle and then finally about the trip up to Santa Croce and what they had seen on Gallinara. He didn't tell the officer about his uncle's hidden room or its contents or anything about the death of his parents and what looked like his uncle's investigation.

Offredi listened in silence, nodding his head now and again and very occasionally interrupting for clarification. When it was clear Ben had finished his story Offredi remained silent looking directly into Ben's eyes as if trying to look into his mind or soul to assess if he was telling the truth. Ben held his gaze but after a few seconds looked away, self conscious under such scrutiny.

The officer cleared his throat. 'I think I know this yacht you speak of. There is a very wealthy man, a biologist, who has been doing some sort of research there. He has been around this coastline for many years now and making something of a name for himself. I do not think that he would have anything to do with your uncle. This man I speak of he is something of a celebrity. He has given plenty of money to the area, investing in it. This does not appear to me to be the work of someone involved in bad deals and kidnapping people.'

'But we know what we saw. We had night vision binoculars, we could see everything that happened.' Offredi raised his eyebrows in surprise at Ben's mention of night vision equipment, thinking on his feet Ben quickly explained that his uncle was also a keen amateur biologist and used them for observing nocturnal animals.

'This man I speak of, Signor Von Moltke, he has a place in Albenga. I will make the enquiry about what he was doing this evening.'

'That's it? You're not going to get round there now with some men? Search his boat? Look for my uncle?' Ben sat forward in his chair incredulous.

'You have no proof that you saw what you say you saw. Your uncle has not been gone for that long and you have told me that his housekeeper says he goes away for work now and again. Forgive me Signor Weir, Ben, but I am not prepared to go knocking on the door of a very wealthy and well known man at,' he tipped his wrist so he could see his watch, '12.40am just on your and your friend's say so. Now if you be so good as to give me your details.' Offredi pulled a pad from one of the desk drawers and took down their names and addresses of where they were staying. He wrote brief notes down concerning the events Ben had described to him, stopping to check the facts a couple of times. When he finished he stood up and held his hand out to Ben making it clear that their meeting was at an end.

'But…' Ben started but was cut off by Offredi stifling a yawn.

'As I have told you there is nothing to be done tonight. I will make sure that Signor von Moltke is interviewed in the morning and I will report back to you at the villa by lunchtime, so please make sure you are going to be home.'

Offredi walked around his desk; arms out wide as if herding geese, he guided the boys firmly towards the door. 'Alessandro!' he shouted and the officer who had first opened the door came racing up the stairs. Offredi spoke to him in a commanding tone and Alessandro nodded in answer. Turning to the boys he scowled and said something gruffly before striding back down to the ground floor. It was clear the boys were meant to follow him.

'Come on,' Richard tugged at Ben's arm, 'we're not going to get any further here.'

Hearing Offredi's office door close firmly behind him, Ben reluctantly had to concede defeat.

Back at the villa Ben threw his crash helmet into the corner of the settee and swore. Richard had been quiet throughout most of the meeting with the police, but now he decided it was time to be rational.

'Look, I've been thinking. If they had shot Simon and killed him they wouldn't have bothered putting him on the yacht. They could have just weighed him down and dumped him in the sea or left him on the island somewhere. So I don't think he's dead.'

The emotion finally erupted out of Ben, 'What are you talking about?' Ben exploded. 'I saw them shoot him. You heard the bang. I saw him fall, not moving. Oh and if he isn't dead does that make everything all right? We don't worry too much about the fact that he has clearly been kidnapped and shot at?' Ben flopped heavily onto the settee, the weight of his body causing the crash helmet to bounce off and hit the marble floor with a loud thud.

'Whoa!' Richard held up both hands. 'Look I'm with you all the way on this, but I'm just trying to see the plain logic of things. We're not getting any help from the police so we need to try and think things through for ourselves.'

'I suppose so. I'm sorry.' Ben looked up and held out his fist. Richard bumped his against it and smiled.

'It's okay mate. Look I've had an idea. Let's grab something to eat and drink and then go up to your uncle's study. If this von Moltke's as famous as that copper said he was then we'll find a cartload of stuff about him. What is it they always say 'know your enemy' or something like that.'

Ben knew Richard was right and was glad to have him around. Richard was thinking clearly and was formulating a strategy, whereas Ben was still caught in the shock and emotion of what had happened to an uncle he felt he was only just getting to really know.

With a plate piled high with sandwiches, a bowl of fruit and two glasses of Camilla's lemonade the boys sat peering at the computer screen. They had only put a small lamp on in the study so the glow of the computer screen made their faces pale and ghost-like.

Richard was right, there was a massive amount of stuff about von Moltke; from a Facebook page and his Tweets, through to scientific papers and conference transactions where he had given speeches. 'That might be a good place to start,' said Ben clicking on von Moltke's company website. They flicked thorough the various pages learning about von Moltke's medical research facility down on London's Southbank. It had just had a massive £60 million refit so the laboratories were state of the art. Part of the money had come from Government grants, since von Moltke had set himself up as one of the public faces of science.

'Look,' said Richard pointing lower down the page they were on. 'You can take tours of the premises *'...see the latest research in action because who knows, you might actually be there when the next big medical breakthrough is made!'* Jeez who writes this crap!'

'He's certainly got a big ego that's for sure. Let's take a look at him.' Ben clicked on a link headed 'Henrik von Moltke', the page loaded slowly section by section so that the face of the man on the boat was slowly revealed, smiling out of the screen directly at them. 'That's him! That's the guy on the boat that was directing things. He's the one who stood over uncle Simon after they'd put him on deck.' Ben's excitement was palpable.

'It looks like your uncle was right with his digging then,' said Richard referring to the notes they had found earlier in the evening.

The boys spent another hour trawling through the Internet; making notes of anything they thought could be useful. Eventually the pull of tiredness was too strong and Ben showed Richard to the spare bedroom.

Ben slept fitfully and groaned when he heard Franco and Camilla going about their chores. He showered quickly and knocked on Richard's door. His friend was already up and dressed, mobile phone in hand.

'Just fielding a million and one messages from the parents. I said Simon still wasn't back so they are insisting on coming up. I've managed to stall them but we've got to go down to the front to meet them for lunch, otherwise my mother will be up here before you can blink.'

Ben waited until his friend had hit 'send' and put his phone in his pocket. 'Listen I've been thinking. I don't think we should say anything to Camilla. She just thinks my uncle's away on some work business and will walk in before you know it.'

Richard shrugged, 'Sure. It's no problem for me not to say anything.'

Camilla welcomed Richard with open arms and lots of gestures, urging him to sit and eat. After a moment's hesitation both boys realised just how hungry they were after all the excitement of the day before, and tucked into a hearty breakfast. Ben took Richard on a tour around the garden where they avoided the topic of Simon and his disappearance. Once they had seen Camilla leave and heard the high-pitched whine of Franco's Vespa, they went back into the house and discussed the information they had pulled together the night before. 'We need to think what we're going to do from now on.' said Ben gravely. 'Let's just say the police here do nothing because this guy's all powerful and has given loads of money to the mayor or something. What happens next?'

Richard had just opened his mouth to speak when the intercom buzzer blasted through the villa from the hallway making both boys jump. Ben raced over to it and pushed the button 'Yes?'

'Er Signor Weir? It is Offredi from the *Polizia*. We spoke last night.'

'Yes, come up to the house.' Ben pushed the button to open the electric gates and waited on the tiled patio in front of the door. Offredi and a second officer got out of their car and followed Ben to the sitting room where

Richard sat perched nervously on the edge of the settee. He stood when the officers entered the room.

'Ah your friend is here too,' Offredi said in heavily accented tones. 'That is good.'

Ben indicated the policemen should sit down and following suit sat expectantly for what news Offredi had come to deliver.

'We have spent the morning with Signor von Moltke in Albenga. He says that he knows nothing of what you speak and that he knows nothing of your uncle.'

'But that's rubbish,' Ben exploded his fists clenched and eyes wide. 'He was there. We saw him. He was on the boat.'

'Please! Let me finish,' Offredi held up a hand to silence Ben, his tone serious and commanding. 'Signor von Moltke said that his yacht had not been taken out of the harbour yesterday at all. It was easy for us to check that by looking at the harbour master's logbook. We have already done this and it was clear that the yacht remained at its berth for all of yesterday. You could not have seen Signor von Moltke or his yacht when you say that you did.'

Ben jumped to his feet, 'He's lying! We both saw it.'

'Signor Weir! Sit down!' Offredi's charm and smile had both disappeared in an instant. 'I can assure you we have taken your complaint seriously. We have followed through, checking the information you have given us. You have no proof of what you claim you saw. Signor von Moltke has proof that his yacht remained in the harbour all day yesterday. You told us yourself that your uncle sometimes goes away on work business. Based on all of those facts we will not be following this any further.' The officer hesitated, his eyes burning into Ben's, 'Unless you have something to actually show us, any further complaints about this or Signor von Moltke will be classed as wasting police time. I believe that is an offence in the UK, it is the same in Italy.'

Ben was about to object. 'Do. I. Make. Myself. Clear?' Offredi had stood up, towering over Ben; his finger jabbed out with every emphasised word. Ben flicked his eyes at Richard who had sat quietly throughout the proceedings; Richard gave a barely perceptible nod of his head.

'Perfectly.' Ben spat the word out.

'Good! We will be leaving now. Have a good day.' Offredi smiled, flashing white teeth that contrasted to his tanned face and dark stubble.

Ben watched the police car pull through the gates and didn't move until he heard the clank of the electronic lock click into place. He was so consumed by anger and frustration that he hadn't heard Richard come to stand behind him.

'Guess we can count them out. It wasn't worth antagonizing them any further. Someone along the line is a big fan of von Moltke or his bank balance and we're just going to keep running into brick walls until we really cheese someone off.'

'Yeah I know, but we know what we saw. If nobody is going to do something we have to do it ourselves.'

'Have you thought what you might do?'

'I'm going back to England. I can't do anything here and we know my uncle's not going to be coming back anytime soon, so there's no point staying here.'

'When will you go back?'

'If I can get a flight for tomorrow…' Ben walked back into the villa and flopped down in one of the armchairs, Richard followed suit.

'How are you going to change your ticket?'

'I have my own money. It's paid into my account from my trust fund.'

'Oh you lucky git!' Richard couldn't hide his excitement of easy money at their age. Ben's scowl made him suddenly remember how Ben had come to have a monthly payment. 'Oh sorry, I…err…didn't mean…'

'It's okay.' Ben looked down at his bare feet and before the silence became too heavy, cleared the lump in his throat and said, 'I reckon I should go on one of those tours of von Moltke's set up, see if I can find anything that might be useful. Those notes we found upstairs seemed to imply my parents' deaths and presumably my uncle's disappearance are all to do with something my father was working on. Perhaps I can find out where von Moltke lives.'

'Sounds a good place to start. Look, my holiday ends next week and then I'll be back in London. Where's Leatherhead again? It's not too far away is it?'

The boys swopped contact details and set to work gathering as much useful information from the computer in Simon's secret room as they could. They then worked out a timetable where Ben would take one of the von Moltke tours and gather as much information as he could before the boys met back in the UK.

While they were working, Richard's phone buzzed. He snatched it up looking at the message on the screen, then glanced down at his watch. 'Oh crap!'

'What is it?'

'We should have met my parents nearly twenty minutes ago at the pizza place by the tower.'

Ben looked at his own watch to double check the time, amazed at how fast the morning had passed without them realizing it. 'Look you go now. I'm going to stay here and see if I can change my plane ticket.'

'Oh thanks, and what do I tell them,' moaned Richard pointing at his phone, the thought of dealing with his parents on his own not sitting very comfortably.

'Tell them I've heard from my uncle and I'm waiting for him to come back but that we have to leave for the UK again, something urgent to do with his business. I'm sure you can make something up.' Richard groaned again, but picked up his phone and sent a text to his parents, which was answered almost immediately. He sighed and stood up reluctantly.

'I've gotta go now, it's either that or have my mother and any cavalry she can muster racing up the hill and beating the door down.'

Ben smiled. Richard moaned about his mum, and she was over bearing at times, but at least he still had a mum. He held back from telling Richard he should be glad of the attention.

The boys said their goodbyes with a date and time fixed for being in touch when they were both back in the UK. Once Ben had watched Richard plodding down the hill and he had disappeared round the first sharp bend, he raced up to the study and sat in front of the computer to change his flight. This was followed by a quick trip down to the tourist information booth on the Viale Gibb next to the impressive, but faded Commune di Alassio government building. The young woman behind the counter was very helpful and Ben soon gathered the information he needed about how to take the train back to Nice airport and was furnished with a print out of the train times.

With everything set he decided to have one last walk around the town. He located the railway station and checked how to buy his ticket. Thankfully the automated ticket machine had an English translation button and Ben heaved a sigh of relief that he wouldn't have to try and buy his ticket from the surly looking man at the kiosk.

As the shadows got longer and a welcome cooling breeze started to blow in off the sea, Ben wandered along the main shopping street pushing through the crowds of people, all of whom seemed to browse but never buy anything. He thought of his uncle as he stood in the queue at Alberto Marchetti to buy an ice cream, '*The best ice cream in all Italy!*' Uncle Simon had said.

Ben made his way back up to the villa trying not to think about losing his uncle as well as his parents. The thought of only having Aunt Evelyn as his remaining family left him cold. He pushed it to the darkest recesses of his mind. He couldn't afford to have thoughts like that. He would find Simon…or at least if it was too late, he would avenge him. He considered what Richard had said. Why had they put Simon on the yacht if they'd just shot him? As Ben walked up the hill the song of the cicadas increased in volume. When he first arrived in Alassio their calling had relaxed him, but now his manufactured positive feeling started to turn into one of unease, as an uncomfortable sense of being watched grew with each step.

Chapter 13

Ben raced across the concourse of Waterloo station. He'd been back from Alassio for a few days and during that time he had been glued to the Internet finding out as much as he could about Dr Henrik von Moltke. His biography was pretty impressive, very much like his own father's, but where David Weir had been all about the science and the advancement of knowledge, von Moltke's seemed to be all about business and financial success.

Aunt Evelyn and he had given each other a wide birth, almost as if they had an unsaid agreement between them to keep out of each other's way. Ben was fine with that. He had other things to occupy him now and Evelyn seemed to have been true to her word, nothing else in the house had changed while Ben had been away. He had decided not to tell her about his uncle, and the only time he almost lost it was when his aunt started to name call Simon for letting Ben travel home from Gatwick airport on his own. If only she knew he'd actually travelled from Nice airport on his own! Ben felt the anger rise quickly, but managed to bite it back and leave the room under the pretense of some weak excuse.

As he left the station and crossed over to the Southbank, Ben checked his watch and cursed the delays on the train line. Some things never change! Nearing the new, almost all glass building shining in the sunlight, he felt in his jacket pocket for the paper ticket he'd printed off. Von Moltke's set up rose majestically from the pavement of the Southbank, its glass front reflecting the street like a mirror image, although Ben squinted he found it hard to see inside the building. The entrance had a glass revolving door, one of the ones that stops if you touch it, its slow movement making you take small, shuffling steps following it round on its incessant circular route.

The door ejected Ben into a large air-conditioned atrium. Everything was smooth lines and hard surfaces except for the exotic plant arrangements that had been placed in positions where they would be most effective. The first three floors had been opened out, so that as Ben looked up he could see up to the bottom of the fourth floor. Glass sided balconies finished off the first three and Ben could see people milling around as they went about their work.

He could see a gathering of what looked like tourists to the side of a large reception desk. People of various ages and nationalities talking excitedly in their small groups and pairs. Others stood looking around, eyes wide as they scanned the new building. Ben suddenly felt quite self-conscious as he opened out the ticket and walked over to a young woman behind the desk. The woman beamed at Ben and almost sang a well-rehearsed welcome, asking how she could help. He smiled back as confidently as he could and passed over the piece of paper explaining that he was there for the 10am tour.

'That's fine sir,' said the woman as she scanned the bar code, placing the ticket on a pile of others, the only untidy thing on the entire stretch of the reception desk. 'If you would like to take a step to the side and join these people, Holly will be with you in just a few minutes.' Ben looked to where the woman indicated, mumbled a 'Thank you' and moved to the side.

While he waited Ben checked his phone as something to do. He didn't want to make eye contact with anybody who might start up a conversation with him. His plan was to hang at the back and take in as much of the building as he could. No doubt Holly had a lot of interesting information to impart, but Ben knew that very little of it would be useful to him and his intentions.

He was brought to attention by the arrival of a tall, slim woman in her early thirties. Her stiletto heels echoing a staccato rhythm on the hard tile floor as she approached them confidently, a broad welcoming smile showing perfect brilliant white teeth.

'Good morning everybody. I presume you are all here for the tour as part of the Public Access to Science initiative? My name's Holly and I will be your tour guide for this morning.' She flicked her head as she looked from face to face making the tumbling curls of her thick blonde hair bounce up and down. 'Let me just make sure we have everybody.' She muttered numbers as she finger counted heads and then referred to a tablet she was carrying.

'All present and correct. That's a good start. Now before we set off I would just like to point out one or two things to you. Please feel free to ask any questions as we go along and I will try to answer everything. I'm afraid that, other than in this concourse, photography and filming are not allowed. I am sure you can appreciate the sensitive nature of some of the work that goes on here. For your own safety please keep up with the group and do not wander off, some areas are restricted to company personnel only. Any questions so far?' The tour was held up as one elderly tourist requested information on the nearest toilet and then headed off in that direction. Upon her return Holly asked everybody to group round in the middle of the concourse where the tour started with a history of the company, facts about the new building and a potted biography of von Moltke himself. After that they made their way to the first floor.

Holly took the group past laboratories filled with white-coated men and women bent over benches as they went about their work. She explained the research each laboratory was concerned with and pointed out various pieces of equipment that were in use and how they worked. The small group of people asked various questions that ranged from ELISA plating, blotting, gene splicing through to what sort of training a person would require to work in that field…and where the nearest toilet on that floor was.

As they moved between corridors and floors it was clear to Ben that what they were seeing was the public face of VM Laboratories and that the main laboratories were behind the scenes. On each floor the group passed several heavy doors that were locked via electronic keypads or had card swipe locks. Screwed to each were white background plaques emblazoned with red lettering saying '*Restricted Access - Authorised Personnel Only.*' Ben scanned all over the corridors looking for surveillance cameras; much to his despair he spotted several on each floor. This was going to be a lot harder than he had anticipated.

It was while Holly was giving a mini-lecture on the application of gene insertion into bacterial DNA plasmids that Ben spotted something that might come in useful. At the end of the corridor a man in a beige uniform was finishing mopping an area of tiled floor. He had headphone buds pushed into his ears and seemed oblivious to what was going on around him, lost in a world of cleaning. Before moving off he bent down, and from the bottom shelf of his cart, took a small yellow A-board sign warning people of the slippery floor. He placed it carefully over the wet area. The cleaner then pushed the cart over to the far side of the corridor in front of one of the security doors. Taking a plastic card from the lanyard that hung around his neck, he swiped it through the reader and entered.

When the tour had first begun Ben had opened the 'Notes' app on his phone and every now and again tapped something in that might be useful. He was just adding information about the cleaner when he was aware that Holly had fallen silent and a small path had parted through the group exposing him to full view.

'Yes, you sir.' Holly said glaring at him. 'If I could finally have your attention. I did say at the start that there is to be no photography or filming, so if you could please put your phone away we can all get on.'

'But I wasn't doing that,' Ben protested, his face flushing bright red. 'I...I was just texting with a mate.'

Holly's lips pursed, her blue eyes hard. 'If you could just put your 'phone in your pocket and leave it there sir!' She watched as Ben sheepishly slid the device into his jeans pocket and looked back up at her. For good measure he held his hands up fingers splayed and smiled. The crowd closed back up again with muttered sounds of '...teenagers!' and '...shouldn't be here if he's not interested...' Holly affixed her brilliant smile and suggested that they go to the next floor.

She seemed to be satisfied with the many 'Oohs' and 'Aahs' that came from the group as they observed scientists going about their work in HAZMAT suits. Holly explained that the work on this floor was of an utmost sensitive nature and that the floor dealt with aspects of infectious diseases and pathogens, hence the need for rigorous safety measures. Holly explained they were due a special treat and pushed a button on a metal panel at the side of the window. One of the scientists came over to the window and spoke through an intercom. Holly explained that he was the project leader and would leave it to him to explain in more detail. To have an actual head scientist interrupting his work to address them was the *pièce de résistance* for most of the group. Ben didn't need to see much more, most of this public face of VM Laboratories was a sham to entertain the public, including all the HAZMAT activity. He wouldn't be surprised if the contents of the various conical flasks and petri dishes were nothing more than coloured water. He knew that he needed to be on the other side of the doors marked for authorized personal only.

Holly called the tour to a conclusion and escorted the group down to the building's concourse fielding questions as they went. As the lift doors opened and they stepped out they were met by von Moltke himself accompanied by a couple of important looking men in expensive suits.

The CEO of the company stopped his conversation and turned to the group. He flicked a stray clump of white hair up off his forehead and smiled openly. 'So Holly, who do we have here? Our latest group of ladies and gentlemen who have been enjoying a tour of our building? Holly blushed, her absolute cool slightly dented by this surprise run in with the big boss man himself.

'Oh yes sir. Everybody, here is the famous Dr von Moltke you have been learning about and who created...well...all of this.' Holly held her arms wide and laughed. Von Molkte stood back slightly and absorbed the adulation of the tour group, scanning each face in turn. Was it Ben's imagination or did his gaze linger for just a fraction of a second longer on him than anyone else. If that was the case von Moltke's mask was instantly back in place.

'Well ladies and gentlemen, I do hope you have enjoyed the tour and that Holly has answered all of your questions. Do please tell your friends about us and of course please feel free to book in again at any time.' With that von Moltke's public duty was done, he politely but assuredly sidestepped the group and entered the lift followed by his colleagues.

Before Ben left for home he walked all around the Southbank. He'd been a few times with his parents, especially to go to the theatre and for the Christmas markets they had there. He wanted to see just how big the VM Laboratories building was. As he skirted down one of the side streets behind the shiny glass monolith, he tried to picture where in the building the tour had taken him and, sure enough, the public had been restricted to a tiny section of it.

During the train journey from Waterloo Ben tried to formulate a plan for getting into the building. If only he could find a way to get through the security doors, there was probably somewhere to duck down and hide until after working hours. The main problem would be getting from the public side to the private side. Ben plugged his earphones into his phone, chose an album at random and let his head slump against the window. He stared out, his eyes not really taking in any of the passing scenery as he ran various scenarios through his head.

The train was just pulling into Epsom station when the sudden vibration of his phone against his leg made him jump. Ben tapped in his pin and a message from Richard flashed up. '*How's the research going? We got back last night. I've still got a couple of weeks left before school starts, so I'm free from tomorrow. Want to do some investigating?*'

Ben sent a brief text back saying he'd just had a tour of von Moltke's building and that he had quite a lot to tell Richard. He suggested they should meet in Covent Garden in a couple of days and they could discuss what they needed to do.

Chapter 14

Simon Weir groaned as he tried to lift his head from the pillow. He slowly swung his legs round feeling the coldness of the tiled floor as his bare feet made contact. His head spun as he sat upright. The thin mattress on the single cot bed did little to soften the wooden slats underneath, not that he had really noticed until now. Each time he'd started to come round during the journey they'd stuck him with another needle full of tranquiliser. He blinked repeatedly as his eyes got used to the surgical glare of the LED spotlights that burned down from the ceiling.

Looking around the room the first thing that struck him was the spartan nature of it. Everything was white; floor, the high ceiling, walls, bed and bedding, table and chair, even down to the plastic crockery and cutlery. The solitary patch of colour in the room was provided by the beige all in one jump suit he had been dressed in. The only other pieces of furniture were a toilet pan and sink in one corner. He stood up and took a step, but had to grab for the corner of the table as the room spun. Cursing to himself he staggered his way to the chair and collapsed into it breathing heavily, the exertion making him feel nauseous, sweat beading on his forehead.

A slight whirring noise caught his attention and Simon peered up into one corner of the ceiling. A camera was tracking around the room. Someone was watching him. He stared back at its single lens eye.

'Mr. Weir. I see you are awake. How lovely of you to give us your attention.' A disjointed, wheedling voice echoed around the room. Simon moved his head as fast as he dared without causing himself to vomit, but couldn't work out where the sound was coming from. 'Now if you wait just one moment I'll come down and see you personally. Don't go away,' the voice chuckled.

Simon swore back at the voice. He stood, more securely this time, and walked from the table to the sink. His legs felt more his own and under his control.

He filled the sink with cold water and, scooping up handfuls, splashed it all over his face, the thick stubble rasping across his fingers. How long was it since he'd been caught? He scooped up another handful of water and swilled his mouth out with it, hawking up thick saliva. Whatever they had used to drug him had left a horrible after effect in his body.

'Well it's nice to see you have managed to get up Mr. Weir.' Simon jumped and whirled round grasping the sink to steady himself. It sounded like the voice was coming from just behind him. He stared open mouthed; one side of his prison room was now clear glass. The white wall had disappeared. He walked over to it and touched it with his fingers.

'Clever isn't it. Thickened glass but when we pass a current through it, it changes, becomes any colour we want it to. In this case white of course. My own laboratories developed it, as I'm sure you know from your extensive research we don't just concern ourselves with medical issues.'

Simon peered out at a brightly lit corridor. A tall, slim man in his fifties stood looking benignly back at him. He had a mane of white hair and was impeccably dressed. Stiff, crisp white shirt, monogramed tie and expensively cut suit. He exuded the confidence and self-belief that money often facilitates. Behind him stood two other men, both dressed in black; one was the heavy from the yacht who had been sent to warn them off, the other was a mountain of a man. A tall, muscular oriental, his head almost disappearing into his shoulders his neck was so thick.

Von Moltke followed Simon's eyes; he waved a hand in the direction of the oriental. 'Oh this is Mr. Tanaka, I am sure that at some point you will become more personally acquainted. He nodded to his left, 'Mr. Casoni I believe you already know.'

'Now I understand you have been gathering rather a lot of information about myself and my company, especially with regard to any business arrangements I might have had with the late Professor David Weir and CordyGen. Is that right?'

'Go to hell,' croaked Simon, his voice hoarse from all the drugging.

'Now that's not really a very helpful attitude and won't get any of us anywhere, least of all you…except a lot of pain that is.'

'You think you're going to get anything out me von Moltke?' Simon challenged.

Von Moltke sighed as if bored already. 'Well if you don't tell us what information you have and where it is stored then I will look at others you might have taken into your confidence. I believe you had a travelling companion when you were in Alassio?'

'You leave him out of it.' Simon's fists bunched at the thought of von Moltke's threat.

'Well either you tell us or we torture you. But I can see you are not impressed by that, maybe another option…you tell us or we torture your nephew. Oh yes, don't look so shocked; you are not the only one capable of research. We know quite a lot about Benjamin. What ever the combination, it will be fun for Mr. Tanaka here but not much fun for either of you I am afraid.'

Von Moltke held his right hand back over his right shoulder and the man he'd called Casoni put a tablet into it. Von Moltke tapped a few times swiping up and down, left and right before turning the tablet to face Simon. The screen had been split into six pictures. The first was of Luxborough House, the other five were of Ben, two in Alassio and the other three clearly in London. In the last he was stood with a group of tourists in a corridor while a smartly dressed woman with long blonde hair seemed to be addressing them.

'Yes, there's quite a lot we know about Benjamin Weir. You on the other hand have been much harder to research,' Von Moltke smiled and looked Simon up and down, 'but as you're here I don't think that matters too much now. I'll have some food and water sent to you, we don't want you losing too much strength for the upcoming few days now do we?'

'Where am I?' Simon demanded.

As if he hadn't heard, Von Moltke passed the tablet back to Casoni and turned to talk to his men, their heads bent together as they spoke in hushed tones.

Simon beat his fist against the glass. 'Where am I? Von Moltke!' he shouted again.

The men turned as a group and started to walk down the corridor. Simon squashed his cheek against the glass so that he could follow the way the men walked. He could see that there were several rooms like his on both sides of the corridor, although they were lit and their corridor walls glass, they didn't seem to be occupied. Directly opposite was a blank white wall; was it like his had been? Hiding some other poor devil trapped in there?

Simon turned away to look around the room, there had to be something that he could make use of to help his situation. When he turned back, the glass had transitioned turning his prison back into four stark white walls. In an explosion of frustration Simon roared loudly as he picked up the white plastic table and threw it hard at the glass wall, dodging to one side as it bounced back narrowly missing him.

Chapter 15

Ben sat outside one of the cafes in Covent Garden waiting for Richard. He was just positioning the table to see if he could balance it on the cobbles to stop it wobbling when a voice made him look up.

'Hey,' Richard was beaming as he pulled out the chair opposite Ben and sat down, dropping his rucksack onto the floor beside him. 'So what have we got? I haven't been able to think of anything else. For once I couldn't wait to get back off holiday.'

Ben hadn't known Richard for long but the sense of relief and reassurance he got from seeing his familiar face was huge. Just the thought of knowing he wasn't on his own trying to find Simon meant a lot to him.

He briefed Richard as to what he had found out about von Moltke. On one of the days before his trip to VM Laboratories Ben had spent hours in the attic going through the boxes of papers Aunt Evelyn had stored up there. Most of them meant nothing to him; research papers full of facts and figures, memos between colleagues discussing results, conference proceedings. However he did find a folder labeled 'VM Laboratories.'

'It looks like von Moltke was trying to collaborate with my father over the genome project for the *Cordyceps* research. He kept offering his laboratories and some of his top scientists but it seems dad didn't want him involved. There are various emails back and forth and also some correspondence between dad and Deputy Director of CordyGen, Charles Gleeson. It looks like Gleeson was trying to get dad to consider involving von Moltke in some way.'

Richard was just about to speak when a waitress came over to their table and asked for the order. When she had gone Richard lent forward, 'So fill me in from the start. What was it your dad was working on and what's this Cordy-thingy?'

'*Cordyceps*. It's a type of parasitic fungus that's in the environment. It infects caterpillars and insects and grows in them until it is ready to reproduce and then it sends out these spore things through the caterpillars' skin, looks like it's got aliens or something bursting out of it.' Ben pulled some pictures up on his phone and passed it across to Richard.

Richard pulled a face, 'Eww! That's gross!'

'Dad was into finding new antibiotics that could be produced from various chemicals the fungus produces as it goes about its business. He'd got some government funding for this project. I don't really understand the science, but they had worked out the genetic code for the whole organism and it looks like dad was trying to isolate the gene for a certain chemical that might have antibiotic properties. If they can isolate it they can then implant the gene into bacteria so that the antibiotic can be mass produced.'

The waitress came back with their coffees and croissants. The boys sat in silence as they watched her place the cups and plates on the table. She gave them a big smile and placed the receipt in front of Richard. 'Erm…' Richard searched frantically through his bag looking worried.

'It's all right. I'll get this,' said Ben reaching across for it. He paid the waitress.

'Thanks. Afraid I didn't come out with that much money on me.'

'No worries.'

'That's impressive.' Richard said as soon as she had gone again. 'I'm assuming there's big money and big kudos if it works, what with all the stuff about antibiotic resistance in the news and what have you.'

'I guess so,' said Ben. 'Maybe this von Moltke was wanting a piece of it or maybe he was doing something similar and wanted to see how dad's lab was doing.'

'You mean a research competition sort of thing?'

Ben nodded. 'Dad's often discussed about scientists getting really angry at each other over publishing things first or poaching ideas and people. A lot of what they produce or publish is linked to money and investments they get on the back of it.'

'Do you think that could go as far as wanting to kill for it?

Ben looked down at his coffee cup as he scooped up the dark brown coffee swirl in the milky froth on the top. 'I suppose it depends on how important the research is or the money to be made from it.'

'So if this von Moltke guy is involved, and it sounds like he might be, then perhaps we have a motive for it?'

'Could be. Whatever the motive is I think we have enough information to show it's even more important that we get a look at his laboratory set up.'

'Perhaps we should just go to the police with all this stuff,' said Richard, a look of concern passing over his face. 'We don't really know what we're doing and with that official report about the forensic investigation at your dad's place…' He left the sentence hanging and both boys sat in silence for a few seconds while they considered it.

'If Uncle Simon had thought it was worth involving the police he'd have done so right from the start. He had enough information to go there himself, but he didn't. There has to be a reason for that. He had a list of names but nothing was written next to them so I don't know if they are related or not. I started to Google some, but the only one of note was Sir Nicholas

Wellenby, who is apparently the Deputy Minister of Defence in the Government, so maybe he's got something to do with it and Uncle Simon was worried of some sort of cover up with the police involved. Charles Gleeson's name's there, but then he was dad's second hand man at CordyGen, and there's email correspondence between Dad and him and von Moltke and him where he's acting on dad's behalf, so I don't know what to make of the list.'

'Perhaps he was just making notes on people he needed to find out a bit more about.'

Ben shrugged, 'Makes sense.'

'So what do you reckon we should do now.'

'I think we should take a tour of VM Laboratories and see if we can get behind the scenes. It's a few days since I went and we could book it in your name this time so they won't suspect anything.

'Cool. I'll have to go in and book it at the reception though, not all of us teenagers have our own credit cards you know.'

Ben looked sheepish, he knew he had a privilege with a generous monthly allowance and didn't like anyone to think he was flaunting it. He could tell by Richard's cheesy grin that he was just joking, but all the same he changed the subject.

'The only thing I'm worried about is if it's the same woman leading the tour, she's bound to recognise me after having a go at me for fiddling with my phone.'

'If it's anything like most places that do these sort of tours there'll be a team who lead them so there's a good chance you'll be okay, plus they see loads of people every day and you're probably just some ignorant chav to her who is long forgotten. Just don't fiddle with your phone, that could be a memory jogger.'

'When's good for you?'

'As soon as possible I suppose. How are you planning to get past the public face of it all?'

Ben showed Richard the notes he'd been making and explained about the cleaner and the security swipe card. 'It's a big gamble but if the cleaner is there again we can try and get the swipe card or make some sort of diversion or something.'

'So it's play that bit by ear then eh?' Ben pulled a face but didn't really have an answer for Richard. He knew his plan had lots of holes in it.

Ben looked at his watch, 'I need to get going soon.'

'Where are you off to?'

'Back to Waterloo and home.'

Richard checked inside his wallet, 'I should just about have enough cash so I'll walk down with you and book the tickets.'

'Get the last tour of the day. Hopefully they'll all go home soon after that.'

The boys made their way from Covent Garden down to the Jubilee Bridge. They'd got half way across the bridge when Richard felt the need to say something, 'You okay?' He'd been sensing Ben's change in mood the closer they got to the Southbank.

Ben stopped walking and stood up straight, he'd been walking along as if the weight of the world was weighing down on his shoulders, pulling him further down to the pavement with each step. He looked along the Thames down towards Parliament and gathered his thoughts, 'Look, you've been great with all this, but you know, you really don't have to do this. I'll probably end up in a load of crap and I don't want to land you in it too.'

'Are you kidding me! This is the most exciting thing that has ever happened to me. Besides, your uncle was good to me and I like him, so if I can help him I want to. You do know you've no choice anyway. I'm booking the tickets so whether you like it or not I'll be on the tour.'

Ben grinned, 'Thanks,' the relief washed over him.

Richard slapped Ben on the shoulder, 'No worries, but if we do end up in trouble, it's all your fault and nothing to do with me!'

Ben really didn't want to do this alone, but as he watched Richard walk off to book the tour, he had a sense of unease coiling around him that he was getting his friend into something which could prove disastrous for both of them.

Chapter 16

'Wow!' Richard stood in the middle of the foyer of the VM Laboratories building looking up. He turned slowly round and round, his mouth open. 'If this is what being a scientist can buy you then remind me to try harder in 'A' level Chemistry!' When he'd booked, Richard had managed to get the last two tickets for the 4.30p.m. tour. He stopped spinning round and looked at Ben. 'This is amazing. How much money has this bloke got?'

'You have to remember it's not all his, most of this probably comes from research grants from various places and Government funding.'

'Even so...'

'Good afternoon everybody, if you are here for the last tour of the day please do gather round now.' Richard was interrupted by a man's voice calling the tour party to order.

Ben bent his head towards Richard 'Thank God for that!' he whispered relieved that they didn't have the ice princess Holly leading the tour.

The tall, slim man introduced himself as Jed, where Holly was all about power dressing and sharp creases, Jed looked like he'd just stepped out of a FatFace shop window with his trendy, smart casual style. He checked the numbers against the data on his tablet and then led the group on the tour. He followed pretty much the same script as Holly but delivered it in a more informal style, which seemed to make people feel they could ask questions more freely. Consequently the tour took a slower pace. Ben tried to hang out at the back, making sure Richard was in front of him.

Finally getting on to the top floor Ben looked down the corridor. He couldn't believe his luck when he spied the cleaner's cart sitting there, the cleaner nowhere in sight. Ben assumed he or she was probably in one of the toilet blocks. He sent up a silent prayer of thanks to his parents when he saw the security key card hanging from its strap on the corner of the cart. As Jed soaked up the gasps of excitement from his audience at being faced with workers in HAZMAT suits, Ben pulled gently at the back of Richard's shirt to get his attention. His friend looked down to the right and nodded slightly. He'd seen the cleaning trolley.

The group slowly made its way down the corridor towards the abandoned trolley. As before they stopped in front of one of the laboratory windows and the lead scientist was invited via the intercom to come over and speak to the assembled public. Ben couldn't believe his luck and thanked whoever had made the toilets such a mess that it was taking the cleaner ages to get their job done.

Both boys, looking as if they were trying to get a better view, edged slowly round the back of the group towards where the cart stood. They now had their backs to it and were just a few feet from the security card. Richard leaned close to Ben and through gritted teeth whispered, 'What now?'

Ben didn't have an answer. This was the one part of the plan that he couldn't work out and in the end was just trusting to chance and opportunity. Before he could admit as much to Richard, Lady Luck waved her magic wand again.

Two members of the tour group were American scientists, and one in particular, a short middle-aged woman with a severe haircut was aggressively challenging a lot of the information Jed and others were giving them. The lead scientist in his HAZMET suit seemed to have particularly invoked her ire for some reason. A heated discussion started to unfold between her, Jed and the scientist. The group was focused on how it would evolve with one or two of them chipping in, baiting either the American woman or the VM Lab employees.

Ben yawned as if he was just another bored teenager putting up with being dragged around the facility. He casually looked left and right and then behind him. Still no cleaner and the cart within reach. He nudged Richard gently. It was now or never. Ben slowly took a couple of steps back until he felt the edge of the cleaning trolley. Glancing down to his left he saw the security key and snatched it up. The discussion was getting more heated and all Jed's attention was focused on the American woman, trying to calm her down and restore some order.

Richard saw that Ben had palmed the key card and, still facing front took a couple of steps back and to the side. His body was now in front of the security door. Ben saw his chance and slid the card through the card reader. He heard a very faint clunk and the door moved slightly as the electronic lock freed it. With one last quick glance to the front Ben saw the coast was clear, he pulled the door open as smoothly as he could and slipped through, Richard followed right on his heels.

Chapter 17

They stood, hearts thundering, expecting all hell to break loose at the security breach, but nothing happened. The corridor facing them was empty and silent.

'We've got to find somewhere to hide as soon as we can.' Ben whispered, his voice edged with panic. He took a few hesitant steps forward.

'Where?' Richard whispered back, fear starting to rise. His eyes were wide with the sudden realisation that they had got behind the scenes at VM Laboratories and now if they were caught they were in real trouble. There was no going back.

'I don't know!' Ben was trying to fight his own rising panic that what had just happened wasn't his best idea. He moved swiftly and quietly down the corridor, his back to the wall like he'd seen in spy films. He stopped suddenly at an intersection when he heard voices. Richard was right behind him and holding onto the back of Ben's shirt. Ben could feel the tremor of nerves in Richard's grip. Thankfully the voices were going away from where they stood. When he couldn't hear them anymore Ben slowly put his head round the corner and took in as much information as he could.

He turned to Richard, 'There's a door just a few feet down to the left marked 'Stairs' and 'Fire Escape'. I reckon it's probably a service staircase, so that might be a good bet to find somewhere quiet.' Richard nodded. Ben looked again and saw the coast was clear.

'Now!' he dashed round the corner, Richard right behind him and pulled on the door handle. It didn't move.

'The key!' Richard hissed hurriedly.

Ben fumbled for the key, his fingers acting like bananas in his panic. After what seemed like an age he finally managed to get it in the right position to slide it through the reader, which was fixed on the wall to the side of the door. There was another soft clunk and the door opened.

They found themselves in a dimly lit, undecorated stairwell. The walls hadn't been finished off like the rest of the building and the bricks and breezeblocks were clearly visible. Wires and cables were grouped together along the walls and ceilings by cable ties rather than being chased into the walls so that they were hidden from view.

'This looks like it could be promising.' Ben tried to sound confident as he started to climb the stairs to a higher level. He reckoned that as the tour ended on the top floor this higher level must be for some sort of maintenance, the likelihood of anyone using it was therefore reduced. He took each step individually; his body taught ready to jump to one side or simply run at the first sign of anybody else. They got to the top landing and were faced with two doors, one of them seemed to lead to the roof; the other was unmarked except for a room number.

'Try this one.' Richard said pointing to the door.

Ben swiped the keycard and the door opened. The room was pitch black and both boys stood stock still holding their breaths, hearts beating as if to burst out of their chests. Nothing happened. Ben could sense Richard searching for something in his small rucksack and a moment later he had to shield his eyes from the glare of the torch light from Richard's phone.

They were in a general-purpose storeroom. Several meters for gas and electricity were along one wall and a huge air conditioning fan was against the far wall, some sort of wide diameter extraction or filter pipe led from it through the wall, presumably venting to the outside. Apart from some cleaning equipment and tools the room was empty. Ben saw a light switch to his left and flicked it on. A yellow glow emanated from one single light bulb hanging from the ceiling, a far cry from the harsh brilliant white light of the modern spotlights that seemed to be fitted throughout the rest of the building.

'What time is it?' asked Ben.

'Just after 5.30.'

'The tour will have finished by now and they should all be starting to go home. I'm amazed that we got away with that. I thought for sure the cleaner would start shouting when they got back to that trolley to find this missing.' Ben held up the security key card by its strap, before winding it up and putting it in his pocket.

'Me too, but I reckon the cleaner doesn't want to admit they messed up and lost the card so perhaps they'll keep quiet about it long enough for us to find something out. We can always just drop it on the floor before we leave.'

'I reckon we'll have to wait in here until mid evening before it's safe to go out and start looking around.'

Richard pulled a face at the thought of having to sit in the room until then. 'Good job I brought these with me then.' He pulled out a pack of sandwiches from his rucksack and opened them up offering one to Ben.

'That's brilliant,' said Ben taking one. 'I never thought to sort anything like that.'

'There's more…' Richard made a show of searching around in his rucksack, pulling faces like a magician trying to find the rabbit in the hat, when he'd milked it for long enough he pulled out a bottle of water. 'I thank you kindly,' He stood and took a bow to the imaginary audience.

'You're mad!' laughed Ben, 'but in the best possible way,' as he held up the half eaten sandwich.

The boys finished the sandwiches and drank some of the water before settling back against one wall, their legs extended. They chatted in low tones keeping an ear out for any hint of activity in the stairwell. Ben kept checking his watch when the anxiety started to bubble up. Although they were both using the chat to keep their minds occupied, Ben's stomach sat in his belly like a hard knot, so far so good, but that didn't guarantee them getting through the evening unscathed.

As the hours ticked by their conversation waned and both boys almost fell into a trance of their own thoughts. After a while Ben was conscious of Richard's breathing becoming deeper and more regular. He turned to look at his friend whose head was tipped back, his eyes closed and a small bubble of saliva blowing in and out between his slightly parted lips. Ben thought about waking him, but reckoned they had at least another half an hour before they should get going, so he let him sleep.

Ben snapped up alert, somewhere far off he'd heard a door close too heavily. Had he been asleep, was it a dream or had a door closing really woken him up? He looked at Richard who seemed oblivious. He made his way silently to the door and pressed his ear up against it. He held his breath, straining his hearing into the silence. The beat of his heart hammered in his ears, almost, but not quite, drowning out the sounds of footsteps on the stairs. They sounded like they were coming stealthily and steadfastly nearer. Ben couldn't work out how many sets of footsteps but it definitely sounded like more than one person. He rushed over to Richard.

'Wha…' Ben clamped his hand over Richard's mouth and put his finger to his lips. Richard's eyes widened in horror as his mind worked in overdrive making the connections of what was wrong. Once he was sure Richard wouldn't start making noises, Ben cleared the distance in a few strides to reach the light switch and plunge them into darkness. He made his way as carefully as he could back to Richard. There was nothing for them to hide behind so they just had to hope that whoever it was exited at another floor. Whether he was aware of it or not Richard had grabbed Ben's arm, his fingers locked around it in a vice like grip.

The soft echo of footsteps came closer; Ben thought they sounded like they were coming up the flight leading to their landing. The low murmur of voices had stopped, the footsteps faded. Silence. Where were they? Had their luck held and whoever it was had disappeared off onto another floor. He kept his eyes trained over to where he thought the door was. It was so dark that, even though his eyes must have adjusted to the light being out, he couldn't see a thing in the room. He took a breath and held it, willing his ears to pick up anything that might give them a hint of what was happening in the stairwell.

Ben was just about to whisper to Richard that he was going to listen at the door when suddenly it burst open violently, slamming back and hitting the wall hard. Ben and Richard both jumped to their feet, backs against the wall but were blinded by the light of several high-powered torches fixing them in their beams. Both the boys had their hands up to their faces trying to peer into the glare as their eyes objected and refused to focus.

Before they knew what was happening, several men rushed into the room and grabbed them both. Ben fought against the men as his arms were brought behind his back and his wrists secured by cable ties. He could hear Richard struggling against his captors, until the sound of a sharp crack of skin against skin resonated through the air and Richard squealed in protest.

The boys, breathing hard, were pushed down to their knees, a man at each side gripping their upper arms firmly.

The torches were turned off plunging them into darkness and a second later the intense yellow glow of the single light bulb snapped on. Now he wasn't dazzled Ben could see more. He lifted his head and the doorway was filled with the huge frame of a Japanese man in a dark grey suit, his hairless head shining with sweat from the exertion of the stairs. He took a step forward and grinned, nodding his head, which rocked back and forth on a neck so thick it almost disappeared into his shoulders. He flexed his hands at his sides, opening and closing his huge fists as if he was fighting against their own urge to be used.

'Let us go!' shouted Ben, red faced as he struggled to stand upright, then groaning as his knees slammed back down into the concrete floor of the room. 'You can't do this to us. Let us go.' He turned to look at Richard whose eyes were wide with fear; his pale face contrasting with the red finger marks that almost glowed like a beacon across his cheek.

'Oh but we can Benjamin Weir,' said a heavily accented voice from behind the gorilla. A tall man in black side stepped from behind the Japanese's broad frame. The Italian from the yacht in Alassio stood in front of Ben.

'You!' Ben looked surprised.

'Surely it is not too much of a shock for you. Perhaps we've overestimated your intelligence after all the snooping you have been doing.'

'Where's your boss, von Moltke?' Ben spat the words out as if just to have them in his mouth left a foul taste. 'And where's my uncle? What have you done to him?'

'All in good time. You will be seeing both of them soon enough. Now perhaps it is time we were introduced. I am Signor Casoni and this,' Casoni indicated the man mountain, 'is Mr. Tanaka.' Tanaka smiled and nodded his head but there was nothing remotely friendly in the face or eyes. Ben stood almost six feet tall and this guy towered over him, he must have been at least six six or six seven. 'And these,' the Italian indicated the rest of the men in the room, 'they don't matter!' dismissing their existence with a flick of his hand. Casoni walked slowly over to the discarded coats and Richard's rucksack. He looked in one of the pockets and took out Richard's wallet. 'Ah Richard Osborne. That must be you.' He prodded Richard hard in his chest. 'Yes, I think you will be of a very great use to us too.'

'Why? What are you going to do to me?' It was the first time Richard had spoken since they were caught, the tremble in his voice gave away how scared he was right now. The Italian leaned in towards him and smiled, laughing when Richard cowered back as far as he could.

'Oh you will find out soon enough Richard Osborne.' Casoni spoke to the men in Italian and they pulled on Ben and Richard's arms bringing them to a standing position. 'And now we go!'

Ben started to struggle against the men holding him. Tanaka took a step forward and grabbed Ben's shirt at the base of his neck. The men at either side melted away as the huge man picked Ben up by the gathered garment with the same ease as if he was putting a cup to his lips. Ben's feet dangled off the ground as Tanaka brought their faces together, his eyes boring into Ben's. 'No!' he said, his voice deep and gruff as if the sound had fought its way up through his thick neck to reach the air. That one word sent a wave of fear running through Ben's body. Tanaka dropped Ben to the ground and turned his back as the men grabbed the boy again. Casoni was smiling from the doorway, when things had settled he led the party down the stairs.

After travelling three flights down Casoni opened one of the stairwell doors and the boys had to squint as they were marched into a brightly lit corridor, passed the glass windows of laboratories, all vacant after working hours. Different coloured lights on digital displays flashed on and off and various coloured liquids whirled in conical flasks as experiments carried on running throughout the night.

In the corridor the boys could walk side-by-side and Richard, taking his chance, whispered quickly to Ben, 'At least we know your uncle is still alive if they are going to let you see him.' Ben didn't get chance to reply, Richard received a sharp thump in his back from the guard behind him. '*Silenzio!*'

After they had gone through a few more doors and corridors Casoni stopped ahead of the party and waited for them to catch up. 'This is where we must part company for now.' A wistful look came over his face, 'What was it your Shakespeare said 'parting is such sweet sorrow', ah *Hamlet* one of my favourites. They all die you know.'

'*Romeo and Juliet* you idiot.'

Casoni scowled at Ben, 'What was that?'

'*Romeo and Juliet*, not *Hamlet*, any fool knows that!'

Casoni pulled a face and shrugged, 'Whatever.'

He spoke in Italian and the men holding Richard started to drag him to the left while those with Ben moved to the right.

'Wait! What…' Ben received a cuff at the side of the head as he started to object.

'Ben!' shouted Richard as he struggled frantically against the men holding him. The boys looked at each other, their eyes full of terror at the prospect of being split up.

Casoni laughed as he put his hand in his jacket pocket and pulled out a small red aerosol. He walked towards Richard 'Oh boys, boys. It is all very touching, but come on, enough already.' He raised the aerosol in front of Richard's face and sent out a spray of mist, the effect of which was to make Richard cough once and then slump down between the two men holding his upper arms. His head hung down limp, his knees buckled.

'Richard!' Ben screamed, his face red, the blood vessels standing out on his temples. He tried to kick out, twisting left and right in a vain attempt to free himself. '*Bastardo!*' swore one of the men holding him as Ben raised his foot and brought his shoe down hard, raking along the length of the man's shin before crushing down on his foot. Casoni leant forward smiling, with his face in Ben's he brought up a finger and wagged it from side to side 'Tut, tut, tut!' He raised the red aerosol and sprayed it in Ben's face. Ben held his breath, but his exertions had left him breathless and, as much as he knew he shouldn't, he had to inhale. As he felt his legs buckle beneath him the last thing Ben saw before everything went black was Richard's limp frame being dragged along the corridor in the opposite direction.

Chapter 18

Slowly Ben started to become aware of his surroundings. Faint buzzing and beeping noises, as if they were several rooms away, invaded his brain. Running over the top of the background noise was a mumble of voices. Men's voices, although too indistinct to be able to make anything out. Ben tried to open his eyes, blinking away the blurred images. Gradually the trousers covering his thighs came into focus, his head was flopped forward, chin resting on his chest. As he came round he became aware of the nagging ache in his neck and shoulders, he tried to swallow, but it felt like his tongue was stuck to the roof of his mouth. Ben slowly lifted his head, wincing at the throbbing in his brain as he did so. He could see banks of monitors and other electrical equipment, desks and chairs, he was dimly aware of the shapes of people, but the crescendo of the pounding in his head instantly felt like a cannon repeat firing. He let out an involuntary groan.

At the sound of his voice a high backed, black chair slowly spun round from a command console. Ben's eyes, drawn to the movement, slowly focused on a grey suit and a man with a shock of white hair, von Moltke smiled at Ben.

'Ah I see our young visitor is finally back with us. Tanaka fetch Master Weir some water, I am sure he must be feeling a tad thirsty after that drug.' Ben was aware of a huge dark shape passing across his vision and a moment later a glass was being held to his lips. He drank greedily, the cold refreshing water reviving his mouth but triggering a coughing fit as it lubricated his throat. Von Moltke looked at Ben with mild disgust as water ran down his chin and dripped onto his shirt. 'Well I suppose that's only to be expected under the circumstances,' he muttered as he reached over to a wheeled trolley and passed Tanaka a paper towel.

'Where…where am I?' croaked Ben, his voice rusty from the effects of being drugged.

'You're still at VM Laboratories,' said von Moltke holding out his hands taking in the room. 'In fact you have arrived just in time to see one of our most exciting trials yet.' Von Moltke gripped his hands in front of him as if in prayer, 'It really is quite a privilege for you Benjamin, this is going to be so exciting, the culmination of several years of work.'

'It's Ben!' Hearing someone like von Moltke use his full name struck a nerve. Since his grandmother had died the only other times he was called 'Benjamin' were by his parents when they were being serious about something, so much so that it had become something of a standing joke.

'Ugh, well if you insist. I think diminutives are so uncouth,' sneered von Moltke. He swivelled his chair around and spoke to the men in white coats who had been monitoring the screens.

Ben moved his head slowly taking in his surroundings. Towards one wall Casoni and a couple of his henchmen stood impassively, like military men at ease awaiting orders, ready to snap into action the minute any command was issued. Something was odd about the wall straight ahead, its white starkness was unusually reflective of the lights in the room, but Ben didn't concern himself with it too much. He was aware of more people stood on the other side of where he sat. He tried to shift his position in the chair, but the nagging pain in his neck and shoulders instantly intensified. His hands had been brought together around the back of the chair and his wrists bound tightly. Gritting his teeth Ben shuffled by degrees until he could see two men in suits. One looked in his sixties, the other was a much younger man, but in Ben's fuzzy mind his face struck a chord of familiarity. Suddenly the realization hit Ben like a steam train.

'You!' His eyes blazed at the younger of the two men who glanced at him and immediately looked away.

At the sudden outburst von Moltke spun round to face Ben and then followed his gaze. 'Oh but of course, you two must know each other. Many apologies, I should have introduced you before. Now, let me see, Mr. Gleeson you know of course, and the other gentleman is Sir Nicholas Wellenby, Deputy Minister for Defence.'

'What's he doing here?' Ben spat.

'Mr. Gleeson?' von Moltke sat back offering the chance for Cordygen's Deputy Director to explain himself. Gleeson looked down at his feet unable to meet the accusing look on Ben's face. 'No? Well in that case let me explain.'

'I wanted to collaborate with your father regarding other uses of the DNA sequencing discovered by his laboratory. I considered that we could work well together through the combined expertise of our laboratories, but your father wasn't interested. He refused all entreaties to collaborate and share the detailed data on sequencing. Of course we could have done it ourselves here at VM Laboratories but quite frankly what is the point of wasting all that time and effort when your father had already done it.'

'My father wouldn't have had anything to do with a mad man like you.' Ben hurled at von Moltke his blue eyes blazing.

'Well it would seem so, which is why Mr. Gleeson here proved to be so useful to me and why your father had to er, how shall I say…be removed.'

Ben turned to Gleeson. 'So you betrayed my father? After all he'd done for you. He believed in you and your ability and was that how you repaid him? To get him killed, him and my mother!'

'It wasn't like that Ben,' the accusations provoked a reaction out of Gleeson who had suddenly become animated. 'We stood to make a lot of money from other applications of the biology of *Cordyceps*; we could have funded a huge amount of research, moved to new premises as good as these, but he wouldn't listen. He was just fixated on the production of a new antibiotic. He wouldn't listen to any discussion.'

'That's because he probably had good reason to distrust you and whatever other uses you were considering.'

'Oh, only the best uses,' interrupted von Moltke, 'the most lucrative of which will be in the field of germ warfare, which is where Sir Nicholas here comes in...but more for selling to the highest bidder rather than altruistic investment for the British government eh Minister?' The Minister cleared his throat; the discomfort at being the centre of attention making the colour rise up his cheeks, he didn't say anything but kept looking forward as if he was not part of the proceedings.

'My father would never agree to anything like that!'

'Right again Benjamin, my we are sharp today aren't we.'

Ben swore at von Moltke who smirked and turned back to the console, leaning his head to one side as one of the white-coated scientists spoke to him. With a flourish he stood, arms extended and turned to face the room.

'Gentlemen! It would seem that we are ready for the trial to begin. This is the first time we have been able to trial the adapted gene sequencing on a test subject larger than a sheep and one for which it is intended. Fingers crossed it is successful!' Von Moltke's eyes shone with anticipation and he beamed with excitement as if he was announcing the first night of his own work at the theatre to an expectant audience.

'Mr. Tanaka, if you please I am sure that Master Weir would like to have a prime viewing position, after all his father did contribute in no small part to what we are about to witness.' Von Moltke indicated a spot close to his own chair.

Ben felt his body lurch as Tanaka grabbed each side of the backrest and pushed it forwards. He was aware of Gleeson, the Minister, Casoni and his henchmen crowding in around him, all peering at the reflective white glass wall.

Von Moltke leaned forward towards the control panel and pushed a series of buttons. The glass wall, that had been opaque, shimmered and cleared. Ben gasped involuntarily.

'Richard!' he shouted at his friend, his legs kicking out as he tried to get to his feet. Tanaka immediately grabbed Ben's shoulders and forced him back onto the chair pressing him down. Struggling against Tanaka's vice like grip Ben managed to turn to von Moltke, 'You bastard! Let him go. He knows nothing at all about why we're here. It's me you want.'

Von Moltke leaned forwards and placed his elbows on his knees, his fingers steepled together in front of his face. He smiled at Ben. 'Oh but you see he has done something wrong. Oh don't look so shocked. I agree his predicament is all down to you, but you see Benjamin, you are the one who led poor Richard here astray and yet it is Richard who is going to pay for it, well for now anyway.' Von Moltke swivelled his chair back to the control panel and started to flick buttons; monitors and screens that had been blank sparked to life, each playing through a slideshow of images. Simon, Ben and Richard on the yacht, Ben and Richard at the villa, Ben and Richard planning their next move at the café in the Piazzetta Fraticappuccini, the pair of them arriving and leaving the police station in Alassio, several of Ben on his own during the VM Labs tour and then finally Richard and Ben on the same tour hours earlier.

'You knew? You knew all the time.' Ben said, the disbelief and shock causing him to deflate into his chair. Tanaka was taking no chances though, his massive hands staying firmly on Ben's shoulders.

Von Moltke smiled smugly, 'Oh please Benjamin. I have an entire security and information-gathering department at my disposal 24 hours a day. You surely didn't think that all your juvenile detecting was going to go unnoticed? Why do you think the cleaner was absent from his trolley for so long? I could have had a three course meal while waiting for you to take your chance there. Why do you think nobody responded to the fifteen security cameras you and your little friend there were tracked on as you scurried about my corridors?' He sat back in his chair and shook his head patronizingly from side to side as if admonishing a small child for a mistake it had made. 'Now I firmly believe that when someone has done something wrong a punishment should ensue. I'm sure your parents brought you up like that? No? Well, no matter.'

'Please,' Ben's voice was almost inaudible, 'I'm begging you, please let Richard go. Don't hurt him.'

'Ah if only it were that simple. You should have thought of the consequences of your actions before you started down this path.' Von Molkte said as he turned to face the front again.

Ben looked back to the window, his heart beating rapidly in his chest, his blood roaring in his ears. Richard was sitting on what looked like a metal-framed hospital bed. He hadn't shown any reaction to the change in the glass wall or Ben's shouting. A thin white plastic covered mattress was all that separated him from the bedframe. This was the only piece of furniture in the room. A series of strong LED spotlights in the ceiling illuminated the room fully. Richard sat with his back pressed against the rails that formed the head of the bed; his arms were wrapped tightly round his knees. His grave pale face scoured the room repeatedly. Apart from a pair of white underpants he was naked.

'Richard!' Ben shouted again. The other boy didn't respond, but continued to hug himself, making his form as small as possible.

'Oh how stupid of me,' crooned von Moltke. 'You know I don't think I will ever get the hang of all these buttons. So many knobs and dials, buttons and switches. The advancements of technology!' he sighed as he flicked two more switches.

Richard looked up suddenly, directly at Ben. It was clear he could now see into the control room. He leapt off the bed and ran to the glass, hitting it with the flat of both his hands.

'Ben! Ben! Help me Ben. What are they going to do to me?' Richard's pleading words echoed around the observation room.

'It's all right Richard. I'm sorry I ever thought to allow you to come along with me. I shouldn't have got you into this. Don't worry. They wouldn't dare do anything to us.' Ben's words tumbled out of his mouth, he wanted so hard to reassure his friend, but didn't really believe in what he was saying.

'Oh so touching! Of course Master Osborne your friend has let you down monumentally. There is nothing he or anyone else can do to change either of your situations now. But…at least you have the knowledge that your contribution to me and my work is huge, and of course I thank you for that, but unfortunately I can't offer you a mention in the scientific paper. I do hope you won't hold it against me?'

Richard launched himself at the area of glass in front of von Moltke and repeatedly hit it screaming swear words with every thump. Ben struggled against Tanaka but he was no match for the big Japanese man.

When the rush of emotion had been extinguished and Richard was left bent over panting from his exertions, von Moltke started to chuckle. Richard stood up straight and looked von Moltke in the face holding his stare, and then he hawked up a huge gob of mucus and spat it at the glass, the force causing it to splatter right where von Moltke's face would have been. Von Moltke was instantly silenced; he watched the strings of mucus slide down the glass for a second before turning to Ben, a look of utter disgust on his face. 'I do hate the uncouth youth of today. Manners maketh the man and all that.' He reached forward again and flicked a couple more switches, the glass instantly dimmed and turned opaque.

'Ben!' shouted Richard, urgently rushing to the fading transparency. Ben shouted back but it was too late, the intercom had been turned off and the friends could no longer see or hear each other.

Von Moltke was just about to speak when a phone buzzed. He picked up the receiver. 'All ready? Excellent,' he glanced over at Ben, 'my guests were just starting to get a little impatient.' He smiled to himself and replaced the receiver gently. He spun his chair and turned fully to face Ben.

'It would seem we are now ready to give you a demonstration of what we have been working on here at VM Laboratories. The trials in other mammal models have been successful, but this will be the ultimate test. We have of course tried it on other human subjects but they have usually been of limited quality, and underlying health issues can subvert true results.' Ben felt a cold chill run through his body, he didn't know what von Moltke was alluding to, but whatever it was, it wasn't good. 'You know those fellows in the laboratory really do deserve a bonus for this, they have been working so hard,' he added, almost as an after thought.

'Mr. Tanaka, this might be something of an emotional experience for Master Weir so I think perhaps he should be restrained a little more tightly in his chair in case he gets over excited.'

Before Ben could react, the pressure from Tanaka's grip increased and one of the minions who had been stood back with Casoni rushed forwards. His wrists pinioned behind the back of the chair were tied to its frame and both his ankles were strapped tightly so Ben couldn't move.

Von Moltke watched coldly, 'I'm sure it's a tad uncomfortable, but you do understand don't you?'

Ben glowered at von Moltke; if only looks could really kill. 'You're stark raving mad!' He turned his head and could just see Gleeson and the Minister out of the corner of his eye, 'And you saw fit to join up with this mad man?' Both men shifted uneasily but continued looking forwards, unable to engage with Ben.

Once Ben's ankles had been secured to the chair, the minion returned to his position and Tanaka stood to one side, huge muscled arms folded across his equally huge muscled chest. 'Oh Tanaka, where are your manners? That's not really on is it?' simpered von Moltke. 'Ben here is our guest and really does deserve a front row seat. He doesn't want to miss anything now does he, after all that's why he and his friend are here…' von Moltke's smile dropped, '…to spy on us!'

Tanaka grabbed the back of Ben's chair and pushed it forwards right up against the glass wall, slamming Ben's knees into it causing him to grunt in pain.

'Now, are we sitting comfortably? Which button was it again? Ah yes, this one I think.' Von Moltke flicked a switch with a flourish and the opacity of the glass cleared again. Richard had sat back down on the bed, a thin pillow behind his back, his knees drawn up to his chest. His pale face wide eyed and wracked with fear. From his reddened, swollen eyes it was clear he'd been crying. He kept looking around the room watching, he sensed danger was coming, but not from where.

'Richard!' shouted Ben struggling against his restraints. He could feel sweat beading on his forehead. 'Richard!' he shouted again as loud as he could, feeling the word rasp over his vocal cords with the force of his scream.

'Now please stop all of that noise or I won't let you watch!' snapped von Moltke. He put an index finger to each temple and made small circular movements. 'I could be getting a headache you know and all that shouting is not helping. Look he can't hear you or see you; the microphone and glass are just one way this time, from him to us. No matter how much you scream and shout he can't hear you. It would be so unseemly to have to gag you, so please, just sit back, relax and enjoy the show.' He pulled a small, brilliant white handkerchief from his suit jacket pocket and wiped it over his brow.

Ben collapsed back into the chair; there was nothing he could do. He turned towards von Moltke, 'Please, we don't know anything; Richard has nothing to do with this. You've got me. Please…please let him go.'

'Oh believe me I would if I could, but…oh if only life were that simple.' Von Moltke gave Ben a wistful smile and without taking his eyes off Ben he flicked the red switch his fingers had been hovering over.

Ben looked back at Richard on the bed; he had lifted his head as if responding to something he'd heard. Scanning the room he seemed to focus his gaze in one top corner. Ben followed the direction of Richard's eyes and watched as three small puffs of what looked like brown smoke belched from the grill of an air vent, the colour disappearing as whatever it was dissipated through the room's atmosphere. Nothing happened for one, two, perhaps even three minutes and Ben was just beginning to think that this was all some sort of sick joke from the depths of von Moltke's warped mind, when Richard started to cough as if he had a small tickle catching in his throat. It quickly escalated and Richard clawed at his mouth and throat as if trying to help the air in. The youth stumbled off the bed as the coughing subsided, only to be replaced by something else as Richard started to scratch his body, his legs, thighs and torso, trying to reach around to his back. Ben watched horrified as small, irregular brownish patches started to appear on Richard's white skin, the patches quickly spread out like ink on blotting paper, smaller ones joining together to form large, expanding islands of discolouration. In panic Richard looked down at his body and started to rub at them as if trying to brush patches of brown dirt off his skin. His movements became more and more frantic as the patches grew in size. At the same time Richard began to moan and cry, the sound rising to a wail as he rubbed, scratched and pulled at his body in desperation. Ben could feel his stomach knotted, his breathing had become shallow and his heart was pounding against his ribcage. He desperately wanted to look away as his friend succumbed to whatever von Moltke had done, but he was transfixed with horror. Tears streamed down his cheeks in silent grief.

'Dear God...' Gleeson left the sentence unfinished.

The brownish patches on Richard's skin started to erupt and Ben could see what looked like some sort of moss or something similar growing out of Richard's flesh. By now Richard had fallen to the floor, his body shuddering involuntarily, the keening wail had diminished to a continual whimper. Within a few minutes Richard's entire body was covered in the moss-like growths. Von Moltke held the handkerchief to his face and was giggling hysterically into it, his eyes wide and maniacal as he watched Richard taken over by whatever he had been infected with. Richard lay silent and still, just his mouth opened and closed as if gasping for air, every now and again his body gave a small involuntary cough and then was still. Small stalks, perhaps six or seven centimetres long, had grown from the brown mossy patches, and as Ben watched the stalks uncurled at their ends revealing a thickened whitish region.

With a sob Ben's head dropped to his chest, defeated. 'Look, look! Wait for it, wait for it…' Ben raised his head at von Moltke's insistence and stared at Richard's body, or rather at the thing his body had been transformed into. The thickened regions at the tips of the stalks started to swell, like balloons filling with air, the outer coverings becoming more and more stretched as the pressure inside built up. Suddenly they burst *en masse* releasing the brownish dust that had first come through the grill of the air vent.

Von Moltke let out a squeal of delight and looked at Ben. 'Pfft!' he said quickly opening the fingers of his clenched fist as if replicating the bursting of the stalks. He threw his head back and laughed. 'I always love that bit.'

One of the white-coated scientists turned to von Moltke,' Seven minutes and forty six seconds sir.'

When von Moltke had calmed down he turned to Gleeson and Wellenby. 'Less than ten minutes, can you believe that? Less than ten minutes from infection to spore release, did you see it? That's our best time yet. We had a fit subject here whose immune function was presumably intact; we have no reason to think otherwise, and still less than ten minutes. Gentlemen I think we now need to discuss what we are going to do with our results and decide how to start mass production.'

Wellenby opened his mouth to speak but von Moltke silenced him with a hand gesture, 'I don't think we should be discussing details in front of our guest here.'

Von Moltke turned to Ben, 'But since we have Benjamin Weir sitting here I feel compelled to say a big, belated and err, posthumous 'Thank you' to Professor Weir for his research files and data.

Von Moltke turned back to the console and picked up the telephone handset 'Get a team to the isolation chamber; we need to collect those spores for further testing. Tell Dr. Pearce I want a full pathology report on the body on my desk by this evening. Oh and the incineration team need to mobilized later too.' He put down the receiver and turned to Gleeson and Wellenby, 'Gentlemen I think we should retire to the boardroom to discuss what we have seen and where we go from here.'

'His name was Richard!'

'I'm sorry? Did you say something?'

'He's not a 'subject' or a 'body', his name was Richard. He was a person. He was my friend!'

'Oh, right, yes.' Von Moltke turned from Ben without another word and again suggested to the two suited men that they should decamp to the boardroom. Ben shuddered and felt the anger rise in him like a volcano. He told himself to keep calm, keep it lidded…for the moment. He would make sure he had chance to express it later.

Ben kept his eyes focused on the room Richard had been kept in. Several people, Ben couldn't tell if they were men or women, had entered the isolation room. They wore full decontamination suits with breathing apparatus. Three of them had what looked like small, hand held vacuum cleaners and were hoovering up the brown dust where it had settled. Two of them were folding out a hazard body bag. As he watched the workers lay the body bag at the side of Richard, Ben could feel the tears welling up; the expanding lump in his throat feeling like it would cause him to gag at any moment. He watched stony faced as they picked up what remained of his friend's body and sealed it in the body bag.

Before he closed the door behind him, von Moltke addressed Ben one last time, 'Well I think this show is well and truly over and we have important work to do. You know the sort of thing, places to go, people to see…populations to infect'. Von Moltke smiled broadly as if he was just getting up from a pleasant beer with friends. 'Oh Mr. Tanaka can you see that Master Weir is settled in his new accommodation, quietly and smoothly'. He winked at the henchman.

Before Ben knew what was happening he was aware of Tanaka's huge bulk towering behind him. A thick muscular arm was placed around his head pulling it to one side and something scratched sharply against the side of his neck. He felt a sudden burst of burning pain and his body stiffened involuntarily before slumping into the chair as Ben sank into unconsciousness.

Chapter 19

'Gentlemen please do take a seat.' Von Moltke indicated the first two seats next to his position at the head of the board table.

Gleeson took a quick step forward so that he could grab the first chair allowing him to sit directly at von Moltke's right hand side. Wellenby took the chair next to him.

'That was fantastic,' gushed Gleeson. 'I knew the alteration of the GYN-J 6q15 gene would speed up the time from infection to spore formation. Tweaking the FTG 9py should also increase spore yield.'

Von Moltke nodded, 'Yes, you were quite right, an invaluable contribution. Work on the FTG 9py is well underway and the latest trials are proving very promising.'

Gleeson puffed his chest out soaking up von Moltke's praise. He was just about to say something more when Wellenby cut across him, tired of his rival's bragging.

'When do you think it will be ready to put forward for full scale trials?'

'I'm glad you asked that Wellenby, because that all depends on the money you can raise from the Government. The next phase will require considerable funding if we are to get it done quickly. Not only do we need to support the costs of further testing, but the design of the launch rockets for the distribution of spores has now been finalized, so we will need to produce them in sufficient numbers. '

'What?' Wellenby erupted, unable to contain himself any longer, 'You've already had eight million from the defence budget. It was hard enough siphoning that off to be transferred over to you. If I try and pass more sideways it will raise an alarm. The last thing we want is some sort of Parliamentary inquiry. There's only a certain amount I can 'lose' from the Ministry coffers before questions start to be asked.'

'Oh come now we both know it's perfectly possible, you just need to squeeze a little bit harder. If you force me to seek outside funding then I will; I'm sure there are plenty of other governments who would be interested, our Russian friends for example. Of course that will be you out of the equation…and surplus to requirements.'

Gleeson sat back in his chair so that von Moltke and Wellenby had a clear view of each other. The self satisfied, smug look on his face showed all too clearly that he was enjoying the minister's discomfort.

'I'll, I'll need time. I might be able to get you some more funding, but I can't authorise it straight away.'

Neither of the men had taken any notice of Tanaka as he had slowly and quietly moved to stand just behind them in the space between their chairs. His huge hands hung limply at his sides with just the slow movement of his fingers flexing and straightening in silent anticipation.

'Sir Nicholas you are not making this at all easy for me. We both need these minor financial adjustments to be made as quickly as possible, and they are just that, minor adjustments. The majority of the hard, time-consuming work has been done. Once we have covered that we can sell to the highest bidder. We will all be exceptionally rich men.' Von Moltke smiled at each of them in turn. Before anyone else could say anything Gleeson sat forward and jumped in, grabbing his chance. 'Dr. von Moltke; Henrik, if I may. At CordyGen we have the facility to make these changes very quickly and we could do it at a fraction of the cost. If Wellenby here is unable to help out with funding perhaps I am able to step in to provide a more suitable and cheaper alternative. I'm sure your generous nature would see my personal share increase appropriately.'

'Now look here I didn't say...' Wellenby started to protest, his voice loud as he turned to face Gleeson straight on.

Von Moltke raised both his hands and cut across the minister. 'Gentlemen, gentlemen please, there is no need to fall out over this. We are all men of the world and I am sure we can sort things out professionally.' Wellenby sat back; spots of sweat beading on his forehead and top lip as if the room was suddenly too hot for him. He tried to hold von Moltke's eyes, but quickly looked away to where the trembling fingers of his right hand absent mindedly picked at a piece of skin on the side of his left thumb nail.

The party gathered around the table was interrupted by a knock on the boardroom door. At von Moltke's bidding the door opened and a short slim, neatly dressed woman, no more than thirty, entered. Her blonde hair was pulled back in a severe bun and her hard grey eyes were cold as she surveyed the four men. Only the slightest tremble of her fingers as she tucked an escaped strand of hair behind her right ear gave away her feeling of nervousness.

'Dr. Pearce! Good of you to take time away from your laboratory and join us.' Von Moltke turned to Gleeson and Wellenby, 'Gentlemen may I introduce Dr. Jacqueline Pearce. We are very lucky to have a world expert in immunology and vaccine development on our team. Dr. Pearce left a very promising career at MIT to come and join us.' The woman looked at the two men and gave a slight nod of her head.

'Please,' said von Moltke indicating a chair next to him on the other side of the table, opposite Gleeson and Wellenby. Pearce sat down on the edge of the seat; her hands folded together, fingers locked on the table in front of her. She looked directly at von Moltke, her face so lacking in emotion it was like a mask, giving nothing away.

'So Dr. Pearce can you give us an update on the results of the latest vaccine trials?'

Jacqueline Pearce held von Moltke's gaze. Her voice was calm, firm and professional, as if she were delivering to a conference on vaccine development. 'The results are very promising. We have tested the current vaccine on eight subjects so far and the last one showed the highest titres of antibody production to the spores we have seen so far. There are also improvements from vaccination to succumbing to the effects of infection too. Just under twenty minutes for sufficient level of antibody to be produced to confer protection.' Von Moltke shifted imperceptibly in his chair. Failing to notice, Dr. Pearce looked at Gleeson and Wellenby and explained further, 'We have been vaccinating subjects and then exposing them to infection at five minute intervals to try and assess how long it takes the vaccine to have a protective effect.'

In a few seconds von Molkte's demeanour had changed, 'Twenty minutes!' he slammed his hand flat on the table making those sat around it jump. 'Twenty minutes! That's useless. We have just seen a case where the time from exposure to death is under ten minutes. What good is having a twenty-minute reaction time to the vaccine? We need almost immediate antibody formation and protection otherwise it's useless.'

'With all due respect, those requiring the vaccine could be vaccinated days before the spores were released. To get an immune response down to the time we have is nothing short of miraculous in itself. As it is we risk provoking severe anaphylactic reactions from both the strength of the antigen we are using and the adjuvants in the vaccine mix.'

'I don't care what your problem or difficulty is Dr. Pearce. I know what I want from that vaccine. It has to be conferring protection in a time less than seven minutes, anything else is failure as far as I am concerned.'

Patches of colour started to rise up the scientist's throat. The shock of the onslaught from von Moltke caused her to blink several times, but she still held his gaze.

'Again with all due respect, the subjects you give me to work with are not really typical for the population as a whole. They are mostly children and severely malnourished with unknown backgrounds. The last test subject could have been anywhere between ten and sixteen years old. Postmortem showed that she also had pulmonary tuberculosis, all of these things will affect the immune response and the results.'

'I want clear results Dr. Pearce not excuses! You should count yourself lucky you have human subjects to trial with and not rats and mice. I have a fit, well-nourished human subject for you to trial with next and the response time will be below seven minutes. You are well paid for success. I can assure you failure will be equally paid in full with the appropriate fee. Do I make myself clear?' Von Moltke's threat was made all the more sinister by the calmness of his voice.

At last Pearce's resolve defeated her and she couldn't hold his look any longer. Swallowing hard she looked down at her interlocking hands where her thumbs stroked nervously over each other. 'Yes, Dr. von Moltke, perfectly clear.' Her voice was little more than a whisper.

Von Moltke sat back in his chair and smiled looking at each person in turn, causing him or her to shuffle uncomfortably in their seats under his gaze. He allowed the silence to last, soaking up his power over them.

'Mr. Gleeson,' said von Moltke at last, jovially turning to the younger man. Gleeson beamed and sat up in his chair. He knew that he was streets ahead of Wellenby, and now Pearce, in his contribution to von Moltke's project and hopefully that meant a bigger piece of the cash prize. 'Do we have all of the CordyGen data on the DNA profile of *Cordyceps?*'

'Yes sir. I've been through all of David Weir's research data now and there is nothing of any consequence that we have missed.'

'Excellent.' Von Moltke rested his chin on the thumb of his right hand and stroked his index finger slowly and rhythmically back and forth across his top lip as if deep in thought. His eyes never left Gleeson who smiled confidently back. 'And the suggestions for the alteration of the FTG 9py gene are also complete.'

'Yes, I passed everything on to your team…' Gleeson raised his eyes to the ceiling as he ran something through his brain, 'nearly a week ago now I think. Based on what we know there is no reason why the alterations shouldn't work.'

'Excellent. You have been most efficient Mr. Gleeson.' Gleeson soaked up the praise; he could almost feel his bank account swelling in anticipation. Finally he had a boss who appreciated him and gave him free rein to work how he wanted, with the added bonus he was going to be so rich at the end of this. Thoughts of what he had just seen happen to Richard Osborne, the deaths of David and Helen Weir and the fate of Simon and Ben were pushed as far as he could to the back of his mind. They had their uses, but they were also blocks on his road to success. He wasn't going to let a little thing like guilt pull him down in his moment of glory.

Von Moltke moved his hand and leant forward, he smiled at Gleeson. 'Then I can offer you my most sincere thanks; you have surpassed expectation. Mr. Tanaka!'

Like a snake striking at its prey Tanaka's arms shot out and his huge hands grabbed either side of Gleeson's head. Almost before the younger man could register what was happening, Tanaka sharply twisted and jerked Gleeson's head firmly to one side. Gleeson's gurgled cry was almost drowned out by the crunching, snapping sound of his neck. Tanaka let go of Gleeson's head with a flourish and the Deputy Director of CordyGen slumped forward across the table, his head twisted round at an unnatural angle so that his lifeless eyes stared open at Sir Nicholas Wellenby. When Tanaka struck, the minister had jumped back, almost falling out of his chair. Now he sat gasping, his eyes wide with fear as he stared at Tanaka's handiwork. He looked from Gleeson to von Moltke and then back to Tanaka. The big Japanese man had taken a step back and stood impassively, his eyes looking to somewhere in the middle distance and all the world like they had nothing to do with the lifeless corpse slumped across the table. Jacqueline Pearce simply stared at Gleeson's corpse, her eyes wide and fixed, but she didn't flinch. It was almost as if some part of her had already accepted the price of any failure.

'Sir Nicholas,' von Moltke sat forward, his face serious, 'I would suggest you do not outlive your usefulness to the project or me. I will expect a transfer of money into VM Laboratories holding account two days from now. I'll make this easy for you; another two million pounds should cover it. I do not care where the money comes from but,' he nodded towards Gleeson, 'for your sake it had better be in the account when I check it.'

Wellenby opened his mouth as if to say something but no words came, his lower jaw rose and fell but he didn't make a sound.

'Sir Nicholas have I made myself perfectly clear?' The minister's eyes flicked from Gleeson to von Moltke, he nodded his head quickly. Von Moltke turned his attention to Jacqueline Pearce, 'Under seven minutes,' he said slowly, clearly enunciating each word. Pearce gave a quick, sharp nod of her head once. 'Good. Mr. Tanaka, will you show the Deputy Minister and Dr. Pearce out please. I am sure Sir Nicholas has a lot of telephone calls to make and a lot of paperwork to complete and Dr. Pearce must be keen to get back to her laboratory. Oh…and get rid of this.' He indicated Gleeson's corpse with a flick of his wrist.

Chapter 20

Ben's eyes flickered open. His head felt like he had been hit several times with a cricket bat. Once again his tongue felt like it was stuck to the roof of his mouth and he had to work it round in order to make enough saliva to swallow. What the hell was that drug they had hit him with? The lighting was bright, surgical almost and everything was white. If anything was ever going to induce a migraine, staying in this room for too long certainly would.

Ben propped himself up on his elbows and squinted against the glare. He lay on a white mattress that had been placed on the floor in one corner of a room devoid of anything except a table and chair, and in another corner a sink and toilet pan. He swung his legs round willing his eyes to focus properly and placed his feet on the floor. Bracing himself against the wall he slowly stood on shaking legs. Almost immediately the room started to spin and his legs felt like they were going to collapse. Ben rested the crown of his head between where the palms of his hands were flat against the wall, with feet well apart he looked down at the floor taking deep breaths, fighting his body's urge to vomit. There was no way he would make it to the toilet and he wasn't going to puke right next to his bed and then smell the stink of it for hours.

Once his mind had cleared, he suddenly remembered Richard and raised his head scanning the walls for anything that looked like an air vent or grill. He heaved a sigh of relief when he didn't see one and stumbled his way to the chair. He flopped heavily into it, waves of nausea still rolling over him. Placing his arms on the tabletop, he rested his head on them and closed his eyes.

Ben didn't know how long he had been like that before a voice came out of nowhere, 'Master Weir, it is good to see you awake. If you look to your left you will see a tray has been placed there for you.'

The hair stood up on Ben's neck and arms at von Moltke's voice. He looked over to the left. Someone had placed a white tray with a bottle of water and a plastic cup against the wall. Ben stared at it.

'After that particular sedative I am sure your mouth is very dry. Please do have a drink, it is perfectly safe. You will see the bottle's plastic seal has not been broken.' Ben considered it for a second. If von Moltke wanted to use him like he had used Richard then he wouldn't want to poison him with anything that might interfere with his precious research data.

He rose slowly to his feet and, one hand keeping contact with the wall, staggered to the tray. He slowly bent to pick up the water bottle. He heard the seal crack and removing the top drank deeply, swilling the water around his mouth.

'That's better, feels good doesn't it?' crooned the madman, 'I'm sure you will soon be feeling much improved once the effect of that drug has completely worn off. Oh and I hope you don't mind the jumpsuit. I know how fashion conscious you young things can be, but it just makes life so much easier.'

It took Ben a second to realise what von Moltke meant, then for the first time he noticed that while he was unconscious he must have been stripped and his clothes replaced with a beige jumpsuit. He refused to give von Moltke the satisfaction of any interaction; instead he stood still and slowly scoured the white room. Von Moltke must be able to see him and there had to be some sort of speaker for the audio, but as much as his eyes flicked over the room's surface he couldn't see anything that might betray the presence of a camera or sound system.

'Stomach feeling a bit more settled? That's good.' von Moltke's voice dripped with false, almost fatherly concern. 'Now I know someone who will be very excited to see you again.'

Ben looked around and then staggered over to where he could just make out a barely perceptible break in the white contour of one wall. His fingertips found a join and deftly traced the outline of a door that was remarkably well disguised. So that was how they got him in the room and brought things in and out. He was not surprised to note the lack of a handle on his side.

'Here you go,' the ethereal voice echoed around the room.

One long white wall shimmered as if its entire substance was starting to melt and then suddenly it was transparent glass. Ben was looking out into a well-lit corridor, directly across from him was another white wall, which, as Ben looked at it, started to shimmer and then clear.

A man in the same sort of beige jumpsuit was sitting with his back to Ben, but as he noticed the change in the wall he turned to face it. Ben's heart leapt and his head swam with disbelief. 'Uncle Simon!' he shouted, his palms flat against the glass, he balled them into fists and started to bang hard shouting his uncle's name over and over. He looked like he hadn't slept for a week, his hair was a mess and his face was covered in thick, dark stubble, but Ben would recognise his uncle anywhere.

Simon had jumped to his feet and was doing the same on his glass. It didn't take him long to realise this was a useless exercise. He stopped banging and waved his hands, shaking his head signaling Ben to stop too. Suddenly exhausted Ben leant his forehead against the glass, his headache momentarily soothed by the cold sensation. He watched as Simon stood back and pointed to his own chest and mouthed the word 'me', then he held up his right hand, fingers outstretched and thumb and forefinger touching making an 'o' signalling he was okay. He then pointed at Ben and mouthed the word 'you'.

Ben touched his own chest and signalled back that he was okay. Ben took the lead this time, he pointed to his eye, then to Simon, Ben made the universal hand sign for a gun that had been made my millions of children for generations and mimed being shot. He then shrugged his shoulders.

Simon signed the shooting back and then put his palms together as if in prayer moving them indicating a pillow and sleep. Ben signalled the thumbs up. He understood what Simon meant. When he saw his uncle get shot it was with a tranquiliser dart rather than a bullet.

Ben felt hot tears prick his eyes and run down his cheeks as he looked at his uncle, relieved that he was unharmed. Simon suddenly stood back from the glass, his face serious, throwing his hands in the air. Ben could see his uncle's mouth working, spit flying as he shouted to the room in general, then it dawned on him, von Moltke must have been using the intercom into Simon's room. Suddenly both Simon's and Ben's glass walls started to shimmer. Ben had a second to see Simon throw his body at the glass looking at his nephew, his eyes wide with fear before the glass became white again obscuring all view.

Ben slid down the glass turning so that his back rested against it as his knees buckled underneath him. He put his arms on his knees and his head fell forward, he didn't fight the tears as they came hard and fast.

Chapter 21

Ben wasn't sure how long he had been alone in the room. He lay on the mattress and stared at the white glass wall as if willing it to change until his eyes became sore, and dry. He desperately wanted to see his uncle again. However long it had been, he'd received two meals, always brought by two men dressed in black. The room would resonate with an instruction to sit at the table with his hands flat on the surface, then when he was in place the door would open. One man would bend and slide the tray in; the second would stand just behind, his eyes never leaving Ben, a semiautomatic machine gun clutched against his chest.

Giving up on the wall he rolled on his back, hands behind his head. He'd only been there a few minutes when he heard a voice telling him to sit at the table; the voice was heavily accented...Casoni! He hated that man almost as much as von Moltke himself. When Ben was in position, the almost invisible door opened and four men dressed in black entered, two with semi automatic machine guns slung over their shoulders and no food tray in sight. This was a different protocol, immediately alarmed Ben stood up. As the chair slid back and he straightened his legs, two of the men rushed at him grabbing his arms firmly. Ben struggled and shouted but he was no match for them. They slammed him face first against a wall and forced his arms behind his back where they were tied together with a cable tie, the edges of the plastic strip biting into his wrists. The men spun him round to face the door and started to push him towards it. Ben struggled, trying to plant his feet resisting their actions, but one of the men who had remained at the door, a tall, solid blonde man with a military style buzz cut who Ben recognised, strode over and slapped him hard across the face. The blow made his head spin and Ben had the familiar metallic taste of blood in his mouth. Before he knew it he was outside the room being frog marched down a narrow corridor.

A few minutes later he found himself back in von Moltke's observation room. The white haired scientist turned round from where he was huddled with other white-coated workers. 'Ah Master Weir, so good of you to join us for another phase of the project. I think it is rather fitting that you should be so intimately involved with this one too.'

Ben suddenly felt cold, his skin instantly turned to gooseflesh, as visions of Richard flashed through his mind. 'What are you going to do to me?' He started to struggle against the men holding him, but his efforts were hardly a challenge to them.

Von Moltke ignored Ben's question and said, 'There's someone here you would like to meet.' For the first time Ben scanned the room properly, his fear had made him fixate just on von Moltke. There was no sign of Tanaka, Gleeson or Wellenby, but Casoni stood leaning against the back wall, the same smug grin on his face. Ben was aware of a chair with its back to him, he could just make out the top of someone's head, black hair messed up. His heart somersaulted as recognition dawned.

'Uncle Simon,' he yelled as he tried to pitch forward towards the chair, almost at the same moment as Ben shouted Casoni kicked out with his foot making contact with one of the chair's arms causing it to spin round. Simon had been strapped in the chair, his wrists and ankles pinned by cable ties and a leather strap had been fastened around his waist. He was blindfolded and what looked like a red rubber ball had been trust between his teeth, held in place by straps that fastened behind his head gagging him.

Ben shouted to his uncle a second time as Casoni sauntered over to Simon and casually ripped off the blindfold. Simon shook his head and blinked trying to focus as his eyes adjusted to the sudden light.

His eyes widened when he saw Ben and he tried to communicate, but his words just came out as a series of grunts and muffled noises. Saliva ran down from the corners of his mouth with the effort.

'So touching, but I'm afraid gentlemen we need to get on, time is money and all that sort of thing.' Both Simon and Ben turned their eyes to von Moltke who puffed out his chest like he was about to give an important lecture.

'Now if we are to have a very valuable weapon here to sell to the highest bidder, we need to be able to protect those we do not wish the spores to affect. I'm sure you can both see how controlling the spread of the spores could be very difficult once released, especially if they were spread as part of a...bomb for example. Once they are picked up by the wind there's no telling where they will end up. Thus the second phase of the project has been to develop a vaccine against the spores should someone get accidentally exposed or infected.'

Simon swore unintelligibly at von Moltke and received a sharp jab in the back of his neck from the stock of a sub machine gun for his effort. Von Moltke carried on regardless, 'Normally a vaccine, once administered to a person, can take days and weeks to provoke enough of an immune response to confer immunity to the individual. Since we have managed to get the infection to spore release time down to below ten minutes you see my problem. We need a vaccine that will confer host immunity fast. It's been a bit of a nightmare to develop, but quite frankly I think we are there now.' Von Moltke stood staring at Ben and Simon, a smile playing across his lips, as if waiting for a round of applause. When none came he carried on undaunted. 'So Ben, you have the honour of being the first healthy human recipient of the new vaccine and the first serious participant in our, somewhat modest trial.'

'What? You're going to vaccinate me then make me breath in those spores?'

Von Moltke nodded. Ben looked to his uncle, his despair clear. Simon was braced against his bindings; if he could, his hands would already be squeezing around von Moltke's throat, but he was powerless to do anything to help his nephew.

Von Moltke clapped his hands and rubbed them together, 'Right let's get started then.' He pushed a button on the console and Tanaka entered the room with two more white-coated scientists pushing wheeled trolleys. The trolleys had trays on the top and arranged along them in perfect lines were hypodermic syringes. What filled Ben with more dread than the hypodermics though was the sight of the miserable, crying child that

Tanaka was shoving before him, his huge hand dwarfing the boy's shoulders. Ben took in the small frame; he looked about eleven or twelve but was clearly undernourished. By his black hair and darker olive skinned complexion he also looked like he might be from the Middle East. His frightened face was streaked with tears and snot. Through sobs he spoke in a language that Ben didn't understand and looked at the adults with wide eyes as if appealing for help from any quarter. Ben looked across at his uncle whose muffled protests were making him red faced. Simon's hard eyes flew from the child to von Moltke and back again.

'Oh yes, you must be wondering. Well we need a placebo too, you know what that is Ben. I'm sure you must have done scientific experiments at that very expensive school of yours with your privileged upbringing. I'm sure they will have taught you about always controlling for variables; well the placebo is something like that in some ways. Anyhow, I'm sure you understand. This boy will do nicely although not an ideal control. Of course his upbringing, level of nutrition and state of health are far below that which you have had the good fortune to experience, but beggars can't be choosers. We need human subjects and Wellenby does a good line in refugee orphans from war torn areas of the Middle East.

Ben couldn't believe what he was hearing. Sudden rage erupted through his body and he kicked out hard at von Moltke, shouting obscenities at the white haired man while fighting to free himself from his guards. The boy started to wail at the scene playing out in front of him. Tanaka held him firm, grinning at Ben's feeble attempts to do something.

'Benjamin!' snapped von Moltke firmly, 'now see what you've done. You're upsetting the boy more than anything else. He has no idea what is happening to him and this experimental run will all be over very soon.'

Ben stopped struggling and shouting. He looked at the boy and accepted that there was nothing they could do. One of the scientists picked up a hypodermic from one of the trays and approached the boy. The child naturally shied away from the needle, his eyes wide with fear. Tanaka roughly pulled up the sleeve of the boy's t-shirt exposing his shoulder and the scientist injected the contents of the syringe into the boy's arm. The child let out a shrill squeal as the needle pierced his flesh and the contents were discharged.

Next it was Ben's turn. The scientist picked up a syringe from the second tray and stepped over to Ben. One of the men holding Ben's arms grabbed the sleeve of the jump suit and pulled it hard, ripping the shoulder seam so that the material fell down towards Ben's tethered writs exposing his shoulder. Ben kept his eyes focused on his uncle as he felt the sharp scratch of the needle and then the weird burning sensation as the cold liquid contents of the syringe were emptied into his body.

'There, that was quite simple wasn't it. Now Mr. Tanaka if you'd be so good.' Von Moltke indicated the door. Tanaka nodded and spun the boy around pushing him out of the room. Von Moltke turned to the control panel and flicking a switch caused the white glass to become transparent. The room that had held Richard was now divided into two. The bed was still in place; the newly created room caused by the dividing wall was completely bare. They watched as a few minutes later the door to that room opened and Tanaka pushed the boy in. Like Richard before him he'd been stripped down to his underpants and, any fight now extinguished, he crouched down on the floor hugging himself, gently moaning as tears ran down his cheeks.

'You absolute monster,' Ben spat at von Moltke. 'It should be you in that room.'

Von Moltke raised one eyebrow and sighed as if any further argument with Ben was just too much effort. He gave a flick of his head towards the door and the men holding Ben started to guide him out of the room. Ben struggled against them, looking at his uncle who was trying to fight against his bonds, impotently shouting against the ball in his mouth. Ben could see bloody marks on Simon's wrists where the cable ties had bitten into his skin as he struggled against them, sweat covered his forehead from his exertions, but there was nothing Simon could do.

'You've got to get him for this. Make him pay! You've got to stop him.' Ben shouted back looking over his shoulder as he was bundled out of the door into the corridor.

The men pushed and dragged Ben along two corridors until they came to a stop in front of a large door that stood proud from the wall. Another white-coated scientist stood there with a clipboard. Without meeting Ben's eyes he wrote something on a form and then pulled a large pair of scissors from his lab coat pocket. With deft movements he cut the jumpsuit from Ben's body leaving him stood there in his pants. The scientist then turned and punched some numbers into an electronic keypad. With a quiet whooshing sound the door opened smoothly revealing a small anteroom and another door. Ben knew this was the air-locked entrance into the room where he had watched Richard die. The group piled into the anteroom where the scientist pushed a button to close the outer door. The guards spun Ben round and he felt the cable tie binding his wrists suddenly give way as the scissors cut through the plastic. The scientist then entered another code into a second electronic pad and the inner door released.

The scientist stood to one side, his eyes cast down at the floor the whole time, as the two men shoved Ben hard into the room. He staggered forward only just keeping his balance, by the time he whirled around the inner door had shut. Ben looked around at the bed and the stark white interior. Slowly he raised his gaze and looked up at the air vent's grill high above his head. His heart was beating fast and he could feel his breath quiver as he sucked in the air.

He looked at the far wall but it remained white, he presumed that von Moltke had altered it so that it only facilitated a one-way view. He tried to ignore the thought that behind that white wall were many pairs of eyes watching him, all of them treating him as if he were nothing more than a laboratory mouse, except for one pair. He knew his uncle would be in absolute despair, but he also knew there was nothing Simon could do about it. There would be no salvation.

Ben walked over to the dividing wall and put his ear against it. He tried to remember whereabouts he had seen the boy crouch down on the floor and positioned himself at that point. He held his breath and listened hard. He could hear him, the faint murmur of the boy's crying filtered through the partition. Ben tried to steady his voice and shouted out to the boy. He told him in

English that it was all right, that he was going to be okay. He didn't know if the boy understood him, but he couldn't just sit there and not do anything. He also didn't know if he was trying to reassure himself just as much as the child. Ben started to talk randomly to the boy, stopping every now and again to listen to see if he was still crying. Ben thought of something else to do, listening at various points along the wall so he was sure where the boy crouched, he knocked on it. A second later came a faint answering knock in reply. Ben knocked again. He hoped that what little he was doing gave the boy an ounce of consolation or even just a simple distraction. Ben heard the boy say something; the inflection in his voice rose towards the end so Ben assumed it was probably a question. Ben told the boy his name; it was as good an answer as any.

He pushed his ear against the dividing wall waiting for a reply, but the silence screamed through the wall at him. Then he heard a sound that made his blood run cold. The boy was coughing; hard choking coughs at first, quickly becoming fainter until they disappeared. Ben sat back against the partition and let his head fall to his chest; he rubbed his cheek against his shoulder wiping away the silent tears that trickled down. He vowed to himself that if he should ever get out of this mess he would kill von Moltke; for his parents, for Richard and for the nameless boy next door.

Ben looked up at the air vent but nothing happened; after he'd been staring at it for five minutes waiting to see the fatal brown cloud emerge, he stood up and went over to the bed. He sat on it with his back to the observation wall. If von Moltke made it two-way he didn't want to look into his uncle's face as he breathed in the brown spore cloud, nor did he want anyone in that room to see his face, to see he'd been crying or that he was terrified by what might happen. Ben tried to push all thoughts of Richard and the boy next door out of his head and focused on the air vent again. His mind raced as he tried to decide what he should do with his limited options. Should he try to hold his breath or get as far away from the vent as possible so he was breathing clean air for as long as he could? Or should he simply breathe deeply and get it over with as quickly as possible?

The whirling of Ben's mind froze abruptly as he heard a soft hissing sound and watched a small, dark brown cloud emerge from the vent. Almost as an involuntary motion he pushed himself backwards across the bed and over the other side away from it. As the brown cloud started to dissipate through the air it was followed by a second and then a third. Ben put his hand up to cover his mouth and nose, but already he could feel his throat tightening and itching as if it had been coated with a fine powder drying the surface of the mucous membrane. The itching quickly became an irritation and he started to cough, he scratched at his throat as his knees buckled and he dropped to the floor. The focus of the room disappeared as his eyes filled with tears from the effort of coughing; a metallic, musty taste filled his mouth. Ben tried to raise his head but a searing pain, as if his head was going to burst apart, sliced straight through it. The last thing he registered was the room flipping upside down before everything went black.

Chapter 22

As Ben started to come round he tried to turn over but his arms and legs resisted his brain's command to move. He opened his eyes and immediately shut them as the bright overhead lights pierced his skull. Was he alive? Didn't he die in that room? Was this heaven? Disjointed thoughts ran through his mind. He let out an involuntary groan.

'He's coming round.'

The voice sounded far off, female, faint. Ben felt something very cold and wet in the crook of his elbow followed by a sharp scratch.

'Aiiee' he said opening his eyes and trying to pull his arm away but it wouldn't move. He looked down his body and saw...skin, normal skin. It wasn't brown and disrupted, covered in stalks tipped with bursting swollen ends. A white-coated female figure wearing a facemask stood hunched over his arm, she took no notice of Ben watching her and instead, concentrated on the vials she was attaching and removing systematically to the needle in one of his veins. Once the vial was full she pulled it off and attached another. Ben watched the dark blood as it was sucked into the vacuum, the plastic steaming up from the heat until the rising blood level swamped it. Once she had taken eight vials of blood she turned her back on him and walked over to another worker, 'These need to get off to immunology immediately.' Ben examined his body again and saw the reason why he couldn't move; black leather straps bound his limbs and torso to the trolley he was lying on.

'Hello.' The woman ignored Ben; he took a deep breath and tried again giving her the benefit of the doubt that she hadn't heard him. 'Excuse me.' He said louder. Still no response. 'You! You who has just taken a load of my blood. Hello!' The effort exhausted him and he dropped his head back onto the slim pillow.

He must have got through to the woman though as she came up to the side of the trolley. Her pale grey eyes above the facemask were cold, emotionless. Ben watched the white material covering her mouth and nose hollow in and puff out as she breathed. From what he could see of it her face was young, ambition carved.

272

'Please, where am I? What are you going to do to me?' he croaked.

The woman's eyes didn't soften. 'We're running a series of tests on you. We need to see how effective the vaccine has been. So far there aren't any visible effects of the *Cordyceps* spore infection, but that doesn't mean to say that there will be a delayed outbreak on your skin.' She was matter of fact, like she was discussing a laboratory rat with a colleague.

'I want to see my uncle. Take me back to that observation room, to von Moltke.' Ben tried to struggle but the straps held him fast. He let out a moan as the pounding in his head magnified.

'I don't know anything about that nor him. My interest in you is purely immunological.' She puffed out her chest a little and her eyes came alive for the first time. 'I am the person who developed the vaccine and this is the first time we have tested its effectiveness on a suitable subject.'

Ben pulled a face. This woman was no better than von Moltke, or Gleeson or any of the others involved in this. He thought about his father and the humanitarian good he did through his research. He was a true scientist, not this woman and her lack of regard for human life in the quest for career advancement.

'What happened to the boy in the other room?'

'What?' asked the woman irritated at the interruption to her thought processes.

'The boy, he was in the next room to me. I got the vaccine, he was given the placebo.'

'You're not very bright are you?' A mocking tone had crept into the woman's voice. 'He was given the placebo. The placebo did its job…precisely nothing and the enhanced *Cordyceps* spores did their job. There was very little to learn from that subject that we already didn't know from previous infection processes.'

'*Previous infection processes?* How many more children have you monsters killed?'

The woman instantly turned away and walked over to a telephone handset on the wall. 'We have all we need from this subject for the moment. We need to keep him under hourly observations and then run scans and bloods in another twenty-four hours. He can be collected now.' Her clipped, precise tone was clinical.

Their encounter over for now, the woman ignored any further attempts at communication from Ben and he was glad when, a few minutes after her phone call, two men arrived and wheeled his trolley away. Watching the spotlights set into the corridor ceiling pass by overhead added to his feelings of nausea so he closed his eyes and retreated into his mind.

Eventually the trolley came to a stop and Ben felt the straps being undone. He didn't have the strength to suddenly spring up and attack the men, so he lay there until a voice told him to get off the trolley. He sat up slowly and looked around. He was back in his old room; a new, neatly folded jump suit sat on the end of the bed. Ben's heart sank as he saw the glass wall was white. He hoped, for all the world, that he might see his uncle across the corridor.

A hand on his back pushed him forwards and he was told again to get off the trolley. He stood on shaky legs and made his way over to the bed. As he turned, the two men were already wheeling the trolley out of the door, within a few seconds he was back on his own. He knew they would be watching his every move, adding to their data sets, again he thought about the millions of mice and rats that lived their lives under observation in small white polythene boxes.

Knocking the jumpsuit on the floor he lay back on the bed. He needed to see his skin, to see if any of it started to discolour, its smooth surface disrupt. Eventually he shut his eyes overcome by the need to sleep.

Chapter 23

Ben got up from the floor breathless and sweating. He'd managed seventy press-ups, any longer in this room and he'd soon be up to a hundred a day. His strength had quickly come back, so partly to keep his stamina and partly to relieve the boredom of being shut up in the room with nothing to do, Ben had worked out an exercise regime. He shook his arms out and then reached up to the ceiling, feeling his body stretch out. He examined his skin for the first time that day, or what he assumed was that day, the lights were never turned out. It was clear, no brown patches. He still refused to wear the jumpsuit, which remained where he had thrown it, in one corner of the room. He flopped back on his bed and looked around. No matter how much he scanned the walls, floor and ceiling, he could not make out where the cameras, microphones and speakers were.

'Come on,' he shouted to the air above him, 'you could at least give me some clean underpants.' He smiled to himself, but seriously it was becoming a concern, they'd reached the stage where they'd be better burnt than washed.

Ben had tried to keep track of the meals he'd been given and if his estimate was right he'd been in the room for six days. His only sight of another living person was when they brought him food or wheeled him, strapped to a trolley, over to the testing rooms where he had blood taken and provided samples of saliva and urine. He was subjected to full body examinations, various scans and X-rays. Everybody refused to engage with him, other than to stick needles in him or position him in machines. Any questions went unacknowledged. After that first time he didn't see the woman who had developed the vaccine again.

It was clear he'd been very lucky, the vaccine had worked for him and soon he would be a hundred per cent fit. Right now he was still providing results and data for them, but what about when they were sure of their results? What would happen then? Ben pushed the thought from his mind. Sit-ups. He needed to start on the next round of his exercise regimen.

In the absence of a bar to latch his toes under, Ben lay on the floor and brought his knees up crossing his feet at the ankles. Hands behind his head Ben curled the top part of his body up, elbows almost hitting his knees. He counted them off in his head.

'Sit at the table.' The voice came as a command, not as a request as it had done many times before. Ben ignored it concentrating on the count; he'd got into his rhythm and could feel the pull in his abdominals developing nicely as the muscles got into their stride. 'You will not receive another warning, sit at the table. Now!'

Ben stopped, 'Jeez Louise!' he shouted and rolled over onto his front pushing himself to his hands and knees before getting up and sitting at the table, he slapped the surface hard with his hands venting some of his frustration. Once, ages ago now, before the vaccine episode, he had ignored a repeated command to sit at the table and several men had rushed in with rubber truncheons and beaten him. He didn't want to experience a repeat.

The door slid open and two men dressed in black entered quickly; a third, submachine gun held at an angle across his chest stood in the doorway. His demeanour was made all the more menacing by the ugly scar that travelled across the bridge of his nose and down under his left eye. Ben hadn't seen any of them before. They worked with silent efficiency, one grabbed his wrists and held them out in front; the other quickly secured a cable tie around them. 'That's different,' Ben thought to himself as he was hauled to his feet and pushed towards the door. Normally his hands were always pinned behind his back. As he reached the door the man with the machine gun turned his back and started to walk away, Ben was shoved from behind, a clear indication to follow him. As soon as the corridor widened enough the two men appeared at Ben's side each firmly gripping his upper arm.

'Ben! Ben, thank God!'

Ben's head snapped up as he stepped through another security door. His uncle was stood between two men who were struggling to hold onto him. 'Uncle Simon!' Ben managed to pull away from his captors before they could secure their hold on him. He ran to his uncle, grabbing hold of the front of his jumpsuit as the men caught him up and tried to pull him away.

'Thank God you're all right Ben. They wouldn't tell me anything. You collapsed and they just took you away. That boy…I couldn't bear the thought of you…'

'I'm fine, their vaccine worked.'

One of the men in black chopped his hand down across Ben's wrists causing him to lose his grip on his uncle. He fought back as they overpowered him and pulled him away. 'Save your strength Ben,' his uncle told him. Ben stopped, his breath coming rapid and hard, his uncle was right. God knows where they were being taken and for what purpose.

Until then the man with the submachine gun had been stood back as if bored by the whole reunion and his colleagues' poor efforts at holding their captives. He stepped in front of them and commanded the party to follow him.

Ben and Simon let themselves be led up three flights of stairs and along several corridors. The scenery changed from dour grey concrete corridor walls to the sterile, bright white of laboratories and onto carpeted floors and walls of colour, decked with photographs and prints. They passed a few workers going about their business, but no one paid them any heed. It was as if they were invisible. Simon unshaven and dishevelled in his beige jumpsuit and Ben just in his dirty pants. Even the man with a semiautomatic held across his chest didn't cause a sideways glance! Surely someone there had a vestige of compassion left. It was as if they had seen it all before, or knew better than to show acknowledgement.

Ben thought he'd almost had a chance to do something when they were passing one of the laboratories. Suddenly, with a soft whooshing sound, one of the security doors that led from the public side of VM Laboratories to the private side opened as a white coat entered. Ben had a glimpse to the outside world. It must be a working weekday judging by the number of people who seemed to be out there and the hubbub that emanated from the open door. Before he had taken it all in and registered his chance though the door had shut.

'Wait here,' Scarface commanded as Simon and Ben stood before one of the identical doors along this corridor. The man passed through the door. From the corner of his eye Ben became aware that Simon kept glancing at him, looking down at his feet he slightly angled his head towards Simon and looked sideways. Simon opened his eyes wide and repeatedly flicked them to a point in front of Ben. He was trying to signal something. Ben moved his shoulders slightly and rolled his head on his neck as if he was stretching casually. The minute he changed his stance he felt the pressure on his arms increase as the men holding him tightened their grip. It was enough for him to glance over to where Simon had indicated and spot an alarm on the wall. That must be what Simon was indicating. As he stood still he felt the pressure of his captors' grips relax slightly, he knew that any second Scarface could come back through that door, so they didn't have much time.

Ben turned to his uncle, 'What do you think they've brought us up here for?'

The man on his right brought his face up close to Ben's so he could smell his stale breath creeping like a toxic cloud, 'Shut your mouth now or I'll shut it for you!' he growled.

He'd hardly finished the threat when Ben smashed his forehead into the man's nose, the momentum throwing him towards the wall taking them all by surprise. The men lost their grip on him and Ben smashed one of his fists into the glass covering the alarm. Instantly an ear splitting siren erupted.

The moment Ben made his move Simon barrelled into one of the men holding him. The entire force of his weight sending him crashing against the wall and then sprawling to the ground, his lungs winded. As the other man reached for him Simon clasped both hands and brought them hard under his chin snapping his head back, he followed through with a knee to the groin.

Simon was just about to spring forward to help Ben who was trying in vain to fight off the two men who had been holding him when the door was snatched open and the barrel of the sub machine gun poked through. The initial sight of his comrades trying to restrain Ben distracted the scar-faced thug holding it. Before he could take in anything further, Simon had grabbed the gun and pulled hard on it forcing its muzzle down. The shock caused the man holding it to squeeze the trigger sending a couple of rounds into the floor. Simon stuck out his foot and tripped him as the man staggered to gain his footing. In one swift motion Simon was on top of him, his knee across the guy's throat as he wrestled the machine gun from his hands.

One of the men fighting to regain control of Ben suddenly realised what was happening and threw himself at Simon, just as he brought up the barrel of the gun and pulled the trigger. The man was thrown backwards as the rounds slamming into his chest reversed his own momentum and sent him sprawling on his back. Ben froze in shock as he looked down at the corpse; Simon spun the gun round and squeezed off a single shot. Ben shifted sideways as the hold on his left arm suddenly disappeared and the other man crashed into the wall and slid down it leaving a red trail.

'Get down,' Simon ordered as he sprang to his feet. Scarface started to push himself up, coughing and holding his throat. Simon reversed the gun and brought the stock down heavily against the top of the man's head. He crumpled without a further sound.

Simon spun round and emptied a couple of rounds into the winded man for good measure. He then raised the gun further down the corridor and fired a single shot smashing another alarm. The entire confrontation had taken just a few seconds to act out. Simon looked back at Ben. 'Get the other alarms, set them all off.'

Ben stared at Simon from where he was crouching; the bloodied corpses of the two men who had been holding him sprawled on either side. He'd never seen his uncle like this before, Simon's face had changed; he had become the hunter. His eyes blazed with a murderous fire and Ben could almost feel the energy that was coursing through his uncle's body.

'Ben!' he shouted, 'Pull yourself together and get those bloody alarms. Smash the glass!'

Ben stood up and looked down the corridor to where his uncle was indicating. He looked around for something to use and grabbed a truncheon from the belt of one of the dead men. Running down the corridor he used the end of it to jab at the protective glass on the alarm cases. A different sound, more like a siren wailing erupted when he smashed the truncheon into a large black alarm shattering its glass cover. Ben assumed this must be some sort of laboratory alarm, maybe for noxious chemicals or fumes. At the far end of the corridor he glanced down out of the window, scores of people were streaming out of the building running across the Southbank towards the river and their fire drill muster points. Breathless and blood still pumping hard from the rush of adrenaline Ben turned back to look down the corridor, but his uncle had gone.

Chapter 24

Ben ran back down the corridor and stopped just before the door, his back flush against the wall. He ignored the bodies on the floor and concentrated on listening for any sounds coming from the room…nothing. He slid down the wall and from a crouching position chanced a quick look into the room. Several chairs were over turned and a courtesy trolley of tea and coffee lay on its side, the brown liquid staining the pale carpet.

He crawled through the doorway slowly, as he passed the open door Ben looked right and saw Casoni's corpse spread-eagled across the floor. A look of shock had replaced the smirk on his face, no doubt related to the single bullet hole in the middle of his forehead. Seeing Casoni's dead body Ben didn't register anything, it was as if a hidden part of him had kicked in. He and his uncle were doing a job; they were stopping von Moltke and escaping. He didn't have to battle emotions that weren't there.

Ben heard faint shouting and a gunshot rang out. He stood slowly and saw that a door in the far corner of the large room was open. It led to a stairwell and Ben could hear the sounds of feet rapidly descending. He peered over the top handrail looking down to the bottom many floors below. The first thing he saw was the back of his uncle's head as Simon leaned over and fired off several rounds from the semi automatic he'd snatched from one of the guards. Simon ducked back as shots further down answered him. Ben just managed to pull back in time as one of them whistled passed his ear and struck the wall behind him, sending a cascade of concrete splinters over his head.

Trying to block out the incessant wail and ringing of the alarms, Ben ducked back into the room and ran to Casoni's body. He flicked back the lapel of Casoni's suit and grabbed the pistol from the shoulder holster. He hesitated briefly feeling the weight of it in his hand before running back to the stairwell. For a short time a few years back he'd been the proud owner of an air rifle and his father had regularly taken him to target practice; that was until Ben had shot a wood pigeon and the rifle had been confiscated. The excuse that the bird was rapidly consuming the raspberry crop not withstanding his parents' wrath.

He started down the stairs at a run keeping close to the wall, stopping at each landing to listen. The evidence of Simon's route was clear. Bullet holes peppered the concrete walls and steps. He heard von Moltke shout something, more gunshots and then the bang of a heavy door. A few seconds later there was a repeat of the heavy door banging, followed by total silence broken only by the noise of his breathing. Ben carried on running down the stairs.

He'd dropped several floors before he suddenly realised that there were no bullet holes or spent cartridges. Slowly he backtracked holding the gun out in front of him. Two floors up he found what he was looking for. The heavy fire door leading from that landing had a single scratch across it where a bullet had grazed through the surface of the wood, becoming embedded in the doorframe. This had to be the source of the door banging he had heard. Von Moltke and Simon were on the other side. He needed to find his uncle.

Gun held up like he had seen in the movies, Ben set his shoulder against the door and slowly started to open it, ready to duck back the first instant any gunfire came his way. When it seemed clear he peered around the door. The brightly lit corridor was empty.

Quickly Ben skirted along the corridor, his back to the wall. He'd never felt like this before. Amazingly his heart rate had steadied itself and his breathing was controlled. Every sense felt like it was working on overdrive. His thought processes and actions were precise, almost innate, like he didn't have to think about them. He could feel the hair on his arms and the back of his neck prickling, as if the energy that was coursing through his body was causing static in the air around him.

At each doorway off the corridor Ben checked the room. All empty. Simon and von Moltke must have gone through the fire doors at the end of the corridor. As he slipped through Ben stopped suddenly when he heard a noise ahead. He held his breath and concentrated on the sound. It was as if a child was trying to stifle sobs. Slowly he crept to the source of the sound. A door stood ajar. Ben listened for a few seconds and then took a step into the room, muscles ready to spring back or drop to the ground at the first sign of any hostility.

He was in a small anteroom, a desk tucked in one corner, looking through an observation window into a cell similar to the one he had been held in. There were several sets of bunk beds, a table and chairs. The furnishings were a little softer than his, but what struck Ben more than anything were the few ramshackle toys that were dotted about. As he scanned the room quickly taking in the detail, he saw a boy of about ten holding a younger girl to his chest trying to get her to be quiet. The boy glanced over to the observation window, his eyes wide with fear and saw Ben looking at him. He pulled the girl closer and tried to sink back out of view behind one of the beds.

Suddenly something struck the window with a loud bang. Ben jumped back and looked cautiously in the direction the object had come from. Another boy about his own age stood defiantly feet apart, a grim determined look on his face. He had one of the chairs on its side, legs pointing out ready to defend himself and his friends; Ben took in the metal waste bin on its side. As he watched, the boy raised the chair and hurled it at the toughened glass. The chair bounced harmlessly to one side, one leg buckled under the seat. A feeling of horror and revulsion gripped Ben as he realised this must be where the refugee children were kept, the children von Moltke and his scientists used as if they were laboratory rats for testing the genetically altered *Cordyceps* spores. He swallowed down the bile that was rising in his throat. There was nothing he could do for them right now, but he would be back. He wouldn't let them suffer the same fate as their friends.

Ben held up his hands to say it was okay, that he wouldn't harm them but the girl screamed in terror. He realised he still had the handgun in his right hand. Ben placed it on the desk and held up his hands again. He smiled trying to make his face as friendly and open as possible. 'It's okay. You're safe now.' He had no idea if they could hear or understand him. He held up his right hand in the universal sign for 'OK' for good measure. The children's demeanour didn't change. Deciding they were safe in the locked room for the moment, Ben retrieved the gun and went in search of his uncle. He passed further along the corridor and through a second set of fire doors.

Ben had just registered the sounds of furniture being over turned and thrown from his left when he had to jump back, as one of the doors exploded into the corridor quickly followed by Simon and Tanaka. The huge Japanese man grabbed Simon by the throat and picked him up smashing his body against the wall. Simon's hands clawed in vain at the thick fingers, trying to prize them away. Simon struck out at the great head and thick neck, but Tanaka seemed to absorb the blows as if being pummelled by a small child. Ben watched in horror as his uncle's feet kicked at the wall trying to get purchase to brace himself, but Tanaka held firm. Simon's face started to change, spittle and froth gathered at the corners of his mouth and his eyes bulged as he fought for breath. His uncle managed to turn his head slightly towards his nephew, that was all Ben needed to spark him into action.

'Let him go!' Ben screamed as authoritatively as he could. He brought the gun up in both hands aiming it at Tanaka's broad back. Tanaka slowly turned his head as if noticing Ben for the first time. A broad grin broke across his face as he cast Simon to one side like a child bored with its toy. Simon collapsed on his back choking and gasping, drawing great lung fulls of air in rasping breaths.

Tanaka turned towards Ben and took a step forwards. Ben squeezed the trigger like he'd been shown with his air rifle, but nothing happened. With a sinking feeling he realised the safety catch must be on. Tanaka laughed and with a roar charged at Ben, his huge hands outstretched ready to grab his teenage body and break it. Ben ducked to one side and the big man crashed into the wall. Ben sprinted to his uncle and held the gun in front of his face, 'The safety?' he was fighting back rapidly rising panic.

Simon's eyes looked unfocused, but he pointed to a small catch with one trembling finger. 'There,' he croaked, his voice almost a rasping sob. Ben flicked the catch and brought the gun up as Tanaka bore down on him. He squeezed the trigger and was instantly rewarded with an ear splitting bang that resonated in the corridor. As the gun bucked in Ben's hand Tanaka's shoulder jerked a fraction later. The Japanese man stopped, a shocked look on his face as the flesh on his shoulder absorbed the bullet. Gritting his teeth he looked back at Ben and the same maniacal grin reappeared as he ran at the youth. Ben instantly adjusted his aim and pulled the trigger a second time, then a third and a fourth as rapidly as he could. The bullets slammed into Tanaka's chest again and again. It took a fifth bullet before the man mountain dropped at Ben's feet, the momentum of his great bulk carrying his dead body forward.

Ben looked down at the man he had just killed. For a split second the horror of taking someone's life made him freeze, but then Simon coughed and brought Ben back to the reality of their situation. Ben dropped on his knees as Simon propped himself up on one elbow. Gripping Simon under one arm and trying to steady him

Ben helped his uncle unsteadily to his feet, 'Come on we've got to get out of here.'

Simon pushed Ben away and stood bent over, his hands on his knees as he coughed and hawked up phlegm. 'No!' he rasped. 'I've got to stop von Moltke.'

'But he's gone. We've got to get out of here, tell the authorities. There are children back there we've got to get out.'

'Von Moltke's gone after the spores. We have to stop him before he can get away with them…or release them. He's mad enough to do anything.'

Chapter 25

Von Moltke raced through corridors, slamming his body into fire doors causing them to bang back against walls. He had to find the spores. All this was for nothing unless they could be found. If he held them then he still had a bargaining chip, a big bargaining chip.

At last he came to the door he was looking for. *Dr. Jacqueline Pearce* in gold lettering stared back at him. Von Moltke grasped the handle and simultaneously put his shoulder against it flinging the door wide open.

Pearce had her large black leather bag open on her desk, she had just dropped several files of data into it when the door burst in and von Moltke almost fell into the room. His eyes were wide, his white hair wild and stuck to the sweat that had formed on his forehead, a gash just under his left eye oozed blood in a thin trickle down his left cheek.

'Going somewhere Dr. Pearce? Jac..que...line. Without applying for my permission for leave?'

The blonde woman masked her alarm and tried to remain calm. 'The sirens...I...we need to evacuate, so I was just taking the most important data with me. You, you startled me.' The woman's hands trembled as she closed the bag and tried to fasten the buckles.

Von Moltke took a couple of steps into the room, his body still covering the doorway. 'Where are they?' he snarled.

'What?' Pearce stepped back putting her desk between them, but further blocking her path to the door.

'The spores you stupid woman!' von Moltke screamed, spittle flying across the room.

'I don't have them here. They're in the restricted access laboratories locked away.' Fear made Pearce's voice shrill.

Von Moltke swore and lunged forwards. Pearce screamed and dodged round the side of her desk making for the door, but von Moltke was too fast. He swung round and grabbed the woman's blouse, ripping it as he pulled her back sharply. He spun the scientist around to face him, her heels slipping on the tiled floor of her office.

'Take me there, now,' he growled, their noses almost touching.

'We've got to get out of here, the alarms. Please let me go.' She started to cry, her ice-cold veneer fracturing at last. She reached up to grasp his wrist pulling at it. Von Moltke slapped her hard across the face splitting her lip.

'You're going nowhere until you've got the spores for me. Now move.' Von Moltke shoved her out of the door and gripping the collar of her blouse forced her in the direction of the laboratories.

When they arrived at Pearce's laboratory, the scientist fumbled through her pockets as von Moltke cursed her. Eventually her fumbling fingers found what she was looking for and she swiped her keycard, the doors gave a soft clunk as the lock released. Von Moltke pushed her hard from behind and she almost fell into the laboratory. As she regained her balance Pearce indicated an airlock door at the far side of the room. 'They're stored in canisters through there.'

Von Moltke grabbed her upper arm hard causing her to gasp in pain. He thrust her against the wall where a keypad and a separate palm reader were in place. 'Open it!' he snarled. Pearce hesitated, 'Now!' screamed her employer, causing her to jump. She keyed in a six-figure code, her fingers shaking and then held her right hand flat against the black screen. Activated by the code, the palm reader sensors registered a hand placed against the glass; a horizontal green bar appeared at the top of the screen and scanned downwards before returning to the top and disappearing. The airlock door gave a slight whoosh sound as the lock opened. Von Moltke grabbed the handle and pulled the door wide. He pushed Pearce in front of him into the airlock where another keypad met them, without waiting to be yelled at Pearce entered a different code. The red display on the keypad turned green and the pair stepped into a small refrigerated room.

Stood along one wall was a long glass cabinet with racks built into it. Silver metal canisters, each about twenty centimetres long, hung from the rack. He hesitated and glared at Pearce. She didn't need to be asked the question on his mind, 'The two canisters on the right, they're from the most recent trials.' Von Moltke shoved the immunologist against the far wall of the room and looked around for something to open the cabinet. Behind him was a laboratory workbench with various pieces of equipment stood on it. He snatched up a heavy based test tube holder by its metal arm and in one movement swung it hard against the glass causing it to shatter. Pearce let out a shriek and covered her face with her arm as shards of glass arced out and skittered across the floor.

Von Moltke tore the two canisters Pearce had indicated from the rack and stuffed them into his pockets. While he was occupied Pearce saw her chance and ran from the far side of the room towards the door. Von Moltke saw the flash of movement out of the corner of his eye and spun round; he brought up the test tube stand at arm's length from his body. In one smooth movement the heavy base crashed into the back of Pearce's skull as she tried to skirt around her boss. She grunted as the metal connected and went crashing down to the floor. As he walked passed her von Moltke placed his foot under her shoulder and flipped her over onto her back. Pearce's eyelids flickered; he hadn't killed her. He smiled to himself as he stepped over her body and pulled the inner door closed behind him, an action that caused it to automatically lock and the refrigeration to kick in again. As he stepped into the laboratory and closed the second airlock door he saw a button labelled '*Decontamination*'. This was one of the safety measures for any inadvertent spore release or contamination. When activated, jets in the ceiling, a little like a conventional sprinkler system, released a strong and toxic anti biological disinfectant dousing the room and its surfaces. Yet another thing he had to be proud of, VM Laboratories had developed it. Von Moltke thought of Pearce lying on the floor and, humming to himself, pushed the button.

As he walked away his thoughts switched to his next move. He had the spores, now all he needed were the vaccines. Thoughts of Benjamin Weir entered his head and he quickly made his way to the observation room where they had conducted the vaccine trial.

Chapter 26

Simon stood up straight and, suddenly overcome with dizziness, grabbed Ben by the shoulder to steady himself. 'This way,' Simon staggered through the smashed doorway and picked up the semi automatic he'd dropped in the fight with Tanaka. The room led onto a series of other rooms that eventually opened on to a parallel corridor, which looked familiar to Ben. It was the corridor that led to the observation room, the one that over looked the rooms for spore release. Ben felt a cold shiver ripple down his back at the memory.

Even over the noise of the alarms Ben and Simon were drawn to the sounds of someone crashing about; furniture over turning and glass breaking as if they were ransacking the room frantically searching for something.

'It's over!' Simon shouted at the kneeling form of the owner of VM Laboratories. Von Moltke got up from where he was scrabbling among papers and phials. His white hair hung down over his face as his head snapped up to see who had spoken.

'You! No, no it's not over!' von Moltke screamed back. 'You think you've won, but I have it.' He delved into his pocket and held up a metal canister. Simon raised the semi automatic to fire, but von Moltke snatched a flask of liquid from a desk and hurled it at Ben and his uncle. In a reflex reaction Ben pushed his uncle over and fell on top of him. Von Moltke grabbed a handful of hypodermic syringes off a trolley and sped from the room. Springing up, Ben was hot on von Moltke's heels as Simon struggled to his feet, the effects of the beating he took from Tanaka still slowing him down.

Ben turned left and right following the mad man down corridors; acting purely on instinct, adrenaline fuelling his muscles, he had no idea what he would do if he caught up with him. Bursting through a set of double doors he was just in time to see von Moltke finish entering a code into a keypad and disappear through a door. Ben slammed into it just as the door locked shut. He pulled frantically at the handle but it wouldn't budge. Pressing his face up to the small glass window in the door nightmare memories raced back through Ben's mind. Von Moltke had reached one of the experimental spore release rooms; the one Ben had been put in when they tested the vaccine. The one Richard had died in. Von Moltke stood in the centre of the room clutching the metal canister to his chest, eyes flicking around the room, perhaps he was realizing his mistake…he had trapped himself.

Searching the corridor Ben found a fire extinguisher. He ripped it off the wall and rushed back to the room occupied by von Moltke. Hoisting it up to shoulder level he smashed the extinguisher hard against the keypad on the wall. As the casing disintegrated sparks jumped out and a small thread of grey smoke emanated from the wiring. 'That should hold you!' Ben said to himself before he turned and retraced his steps back to the observation room.

Chapter 27

As Ben entered he saw Simon sat in von Moltke's chair staring at his adversary. His uncle had managed to find the correct buttons on the control panel to make the viewing glass two way. Von Moltke peered back at him laughing. He was holding up an identical metal canister in each hand grinning from ear to ear like a father who had just pulled the birthday boy's surprise from behind his back.

'I told you; you think you've won? You think I'm trapped in here?' von Moltke laughed, 'It's all part of my new plan. Of course you've caused me a few problems, but…' he shrugged his shoulders theatrically, 'no matter, as we know in science…adaptation is the key to success.'

'Give it up von Moltke. You're not going anywhere. This place is going to be swarming with agents soon.'

'Good! I'm pleased to hear it. The more the merrier.'

Simon sat forward puzzled as to what von Moltke had in mind. 'You see,' carried on the mad man with a nod of his head, 'these vents can be reversed. Usually we cycle clean air in through them, but a quick alteration via the control panel here and the direction of air flow moves in the opposite direction…carrying spores out into the building and beyond…for you all to breathe in.' Von Moltke walked over to the wall nearest the door and flipped down a white panel covering, which revealed a series of lights, buttons and switches. Ben's mouth opened in surprise, he'd been locked in that room, he'd examined it as carefully as he could during the vaccine trial, but he hadn't spotted the control panel cover.

Von Moltke set the canisters on the ground and half turning back to Simon and Ben smiled at them. He gave a dramatic flourish with both hands as if he was about to play a classical concerto on a grand piano and then turned back to the panel. He pushed buttons in quick succession and finally flicked one of the switches.

Immediately the control panel in front of Ben and Simon lit up.

'Damn!' exclaimed Simon. 'We've got to override this somehow.'

Von Moltke slowly bent to pick up the canisters. 'Wait,' shouted Simon, 'if you release the spores now you'll infect yourself. You'll die like everybody else.'

Von Moltke stopped, his mouth open in surprise, he tutted and smiled, 'Oh yes, thank you for reminding me.' He walked over to the bed and laid the canisters reverentially on the thin mattress. He took off his jacket and folded it neatly placing it next to the metal tubes.

Simon looked at Ben and whispered, 'I'll try and stall him, you see if you can switch that air vent off.' Ben nodded, his face grave as he bent down over the control desk concentrating on the ventilation section.

As Von Moltke swaggered over to the observation window he rolled up each of his sleeves. His once pristine white cotton shirt now creased and stained with sweat, grime and spots of blood. He looked through the glass at Simon, his lips drawn back in an expression half way between a snarl and a smile. Simon stared back unblinking, waiting for von Moltke's next move. The white haired man reached into his trouser pocket and held out his hand palm up. A white syringe lay on it, the needle covered with a purple cap. 'Silly me, almost forgot the most vital component. You see, I vaccinate myself, then hang on for ten minutes, we can have a little chat, then when the vaccine has provoked enough antibody formation I release the spores and you, well…poof, you add to the general spore release that is going to get me the attention I require. Once *Cordyceps* has done its job, I can be out of here and selling to the highest bidder. It's not quite how I planned it but what the heck, the publicity is going to be awesome just the same. It's a pity that odious brat of a nephew of yours is now immune, but there are more ways to skin a cat.'

Simon watched as von Moltke edged his sleeve up far enough to reveal his upper arm. He raised the purple needle cap to his lips and gripped the end between his teeth. He pulled his hand back to free the needle then spat the plastic cover on the floor. Smiling once more at Simon he injected the contents of the syringe into the muscle of his upper arm. 'There we go; that wasn't too bad.' He casually threw the empty syringe over his head and as it clattered off the wall to the floor he rubbed the injection site vigorously. 'Now Mr. Weir, what should we chat about?'

Simon looked over to Ben, 'Getting anywhere?' he said, his voice low.

'Nope, but it looks like these gauges tell us the direction of the airflow through the vents. I've tried to reverse them but he seems to have some sort of master override or something like that.'

'There's got to be some sort of key control that is a main shut down point, it has to be a basic safety feature to stop things escaping bearing in mind the type of work they do here.'

Simon slid off his chair to his knees and bent under the control panel. 'Hand me that spatula.' He pointed to the bottom tier of a wheeled trolley. In seconds Simon had flipped plastic screw covers off and was busily unscrewing a side panel of the control console. A few seconds later he prized the panel away from the front revealing more lights, buttons and wires. 'Keep that fool distracted,' he growled at Ben.

Ben looked over the top of the control desk and saw von Moltke peering back at him. 'Having fun down there are we? It's a pity I can't come round and join the party but…well, you know…'

'That vaccine might not work. You're taking a huge chance. Not everyone responds to a vaccine; some people need boosters and some people just don't react at all. If you release those spores there's a good chance you might still die from the infection.' It was all Ben could think of to try and keep von Moltke's attention.

Von Moltke shrieked in surprise, his eyes wide. 'I'm impressed! Teach you that at school did they? My, my you must go to a good one to have that sort of thing on the curriculum. In normal circumstances you are of course quite right, but don't forget this is a "super vaccine" if you will. It provokes the immune system so strongly that the problem of non-responders is really not an issue. I will be immune, I have complete confidence in the late Dr. Pearce's achievements.'

Ben gasped in shock as he remembered the ice queen scientist who had subjected him to various tests. So she was dead. He remembered the way she had treated him and her casual disregard for the life of the refugee boy, any hint of sadness he might have felt for her death evaporated quickly.

'Well you're not showing any signs of illness.'

'What do you mean?' von Moltke's confidence stuttered for a second.

'When I was given the vaccine and my body was responding I started to feel ill, fever, coughing. You're not doing anything. You look almost normal.'

Von Moltke's face changed as he took in Ben's words and analysed them. Ben desperately wanted to get down under the control desk and ask his uncle how he was doing. He was fast running out of stalling tactics. He held von Moltke's gaze though, silently challenging him. Slowly the corners of von Moltke's mouth started to curl up until he was grinning like the mad man he had become. He stroked his sweat-slicked hair back off his face and raised his eyebrows knowingly.

'You have a lot to learn Benjamin. It's a pity we couldn't have worked together. I think you may have inherited some of your parents' flair for the sciences.

Who knows, perhaps under other circumstances you could have been an apprentice, I could have taught you all I know. You see you made me think you had a point for a second, but the difference between us is that you are still a child and I am adult. We hadn't had chance to trial the vaccine in adults. When the vaccine is faced with a strong fully matured immune system I am sure we would see an equally strong response without any signs or symptoms. Not so in the case of an immature immune system in a child, because that's all you are really. An irritating, boring, stupid child.' Von Moltke's smile had changed into a snarl, spittle gathered at the corners of his mouth and his eyes bored into Ben's. Ben swallowed hard and felt a cold hand of fear wrap around his heart.

'Enough!' shouted von Moltke as he stalked over to the bed and grabbed one of the silver canisters.

'Uncle Simon,' Ben's voice quavered with fear, 'Uncle Simon he's going to do it.' He felt the panic rising, the hairs on his arms standing on end, his heart thumping in his chest.

Simon appeared from under the control desk, grunting at the effort of getting back to his feet. He slumped back down into von Moltke's chair. 'Hey you, Moltke the mad man.'

Von Moltke spun round. 'What did you say? Don't you dare abuse me! Do you know who I am?'

'Well that got your attention.' Ben watched incredulous as Simon sat back in the chair making himself as comfortable as he could.

'Uncle Simon what are you…' Simon held his hand up at Ben silencing him.

'You see von Moltke, I think you're full of crap. A pathetic little scientist who wants to rule the world, but your science is poor. I don't think you've got anything there that is capable of doing what you say it will. You're a failure and I think this will fail too.' Simon was deliberately provoking von Moltke. 'Go ahead release your spores. I'm sick of fighting against you, especially when I think you're full of hot air. So go on, open the top, shake them about. Do your worst.'

Ben looked in panic from his uncle to von Moltke. He looked down at the control panel. The lights were showing that the vents were still extracting air from the chamber to the outside. 'What are you doing?' he asked his uncle, the despair in his voice almost palpable. He fought back the tears that were just starting to prick at his eyes.

If he still had an ounce of reason left it was at that point that von Moltke lost it. He exploded in a fury of temper, his face red, spit flying as he ranted and shouted abuse at Simon. As the energy of his outburst left him von Moltke stomped over to the control panel and checked the vents. He started laughing manically as he twisted the top off the first silver canister and began to flick the contents in great arcs above his head towards the vents. Plumes of dark powder dispersed through the air and slowly fell to the ground like a dirty mist descending. Immediately Ben realised that none of it was being drawn up to the metal grill on the air vent. In his confusion he looked at his uncle who was watching von Moltke intently, his eyes fixed to the scientist, a knowing smile playing across his lips.

Von Moltke threw the empty canister and rushed over to the bed grabbing the second one. 'Noooooo,' he screamed as he looked at the spores drifting down to the floor covering everything with a dark dust. He ripped off the top of the second canister and spun around spreading the contents through the air.

He watched in silence as the cloud of spores rose up and then floated downwards. 'No!' he screamed and rushed at the glass separating him from the observation room, he banged hard on it with both fists. 'What have you done?' he wailed. Brown streaks appeared on his face as his sweat ran through the fine covering of dust that had settled over his skin. Von Moltke bent over as a coughing fit wracked his body. He staggered back a few paces groaning. Ben watched in horror as von Moltke started to claw at his shirt ripping it from his body. The scientist wailed his protest as dark brown patches started to appear on his skin. As all three of them watched the patches grew larger, smaller ones merging with their neighbours. Von Moltke rubbed at them frantically as if trying to remove the stains. He threw himself at the glass again. 'Help...me,' he pleaded pathetically.

Ben stared, barely breathing, as the brown patches started to thicken and the smooth surface of Von Moltke's skin split, unable to contain the erupting fungus underneath. He swallowed hard feeling the lump in his throat bob up and down. Both he and his uncle were glued to the action playing out in front of them.

Von Moltke dropped to the floor moaning, sounds more than words. His movements became more and more feeble as globe tipped projections started to grow from his skin. His legs looked several times bigger as the projections swelled under the confines of his trousers. For a few seconds it was as if all time stood still, then suddenly the glass was splattered with thick brown dust as the spore capsules burst simultaneously.

'Pfft!' said Simon quietly, his voice devoid of all emotion.

Chapter 28

As the spores settled, Ben stared horrified at the brown mass that was once von Moltke. The tears that had been threatening to flow came and rolled silently down his cheeks, falling to the floor as he thought of Richard. He'd shut his friend's death away while he tried to fight for his own survival, but seeing von Moltke die brought it all back in a tidal wave.

'Come on, there'll be time for that later. We've got to get out of here.' Simon struggled to his feet and stood looking at Ben. He was gripping his side, breathing in rapid short shallow breaths. 'Ben come on, we haven't got time for this now.'

'No!' he objected emphatically. He sniffed heavily, wiping snot away with his sleeve. 'What did you do down there? It was like you knew what would happen. Tell me.'

Simon sighed, his eyes screwing up as a wave of pain ran through him. 'I managed to turn off the vents completely, but with a little bit of rewiring I was able to keep the relevant indicators showing that the vents were drawing air out. Listen.' They stood in complete silence for a few seconds. In the drama that had played out Ben hadn't noticed that the faint hum of the air vents had disappeared and nor had von Moltke.

'And him?' Ben nodded towards the dark, smut-covered glass.

'Look at the trolleys.'

Ben turned to look behind him where Simon indicated. The top shelves of the two trolleys were still loaded with hypodermics; one with purple caps over the needles, the second with blue protective caps. Ben went over to the trays and picked up one of the syringes with a purple cap, he read the label on the barrel of the syringe. The various codes meant nothing to him, but one word he did understand, *Placebo*. He looked at his uncle.

'In his madness he picked up the wrong syringe. The blue-capped ones are the vaccines; he injected himself with nothing more than saline or something like that. I saw the difference when they injected you and the boy in here.'

'So you knew what would happen when he released the spores. You goaded him into doing it. You knew he would be infected and...' Ben left the sentence unfinished but looked over to the glass.

'It's nothing more than he deserved. You saw what he did to those children, to your friend.' He hesitated for a second then said quietly, 'Remember also Ben, we're talking about the man who killed your parents.'

'Killing him doesn't make that right. It doesn't change anything. It doesn't bring any of them back.'

'The world is a better place without him. Look at what he was trying to do.'

'But...'

'Enough Ben!' Simon had never spoken to his nephew with such force before. 'We have to get out of here now. There will be a specialist clean up team in here anytime. Most of this stuff needs to be destroyed. All record of the research eradicated so that no one else can take advantage of it. We don't want to be here when they start spraying chemicals around.' Without waiting for any response Simon walked slowly over to one of the wall mounted phones. He dialed a number and spoke briefly into the receiver.

When he finished he turned to Ben who was still staring at the observation window. 'You might be okay, but I could sure do with a hand here,' he said through gritted teeth, bracing himself against the wall with one arm while hugging his ribs with the other.

Seeing his uncle struggling to stay upright snapped Ben out of his thoughts. He raced over, putting his arm round the older man helping to take some of his weight.

'We need to make our way out the back.'

They started down one of the corridors when Ben suddenly stopped, causing his uncle to groan in pain. 'Wait, there's a room back there with children in it, three I think. There could be others. We've got to get them.'

'We can't do anything for them right now Ben. The safest place for them right now will be in the rooms they're locked in. Agents will be coming in the back way along with the clean up team. They'll pick up any children and look after them.'

Ben had to trust his uncle, he'd been right about most things so far. They moved as quickly as Simon could manage and made their way to the building's loading bay. As uncle and nephew limped through the door they were suddenly bathed in bright light that made both Ben and his uncle shield their eyes, the brilliance from the spotlights stopping them seeing anything.

'Stay exactly where you are,' a voice commanded through a loud speaker. Ben could hear activity, people moving about, instructions being shouted, equipment being moved. As his eyes grew accustomed to the light he could make out many people milling about. They were either dressed in white HAZMAT suits with full-face visors or in black military suits, semi automatics in hand and faces covered with gas masks. People rushed passed them, pushing through the doorway into the building, some carrying metal cases and other pieces of equipment Ben didn't recognise. Across the loading bay Ben could see a long tent had been set up at one end, a series of metal pipes and tubes ran into it from two small lorries that had been backed in through the huge doors. For the first time since he had been marched from his holding cell, Ben was suddenly aware that he was just standing there in his dirty underwear. He felt small and very vulnerable.

'It's okay Ben, these are the good guys,' said his uncle as two HAZMAT suited individuals grabbed him, he couldn't tell if they were men or women. Two more took Simon by the arms. Ben stopped struggling and allowed himself to be led towards the long tent, he glanced over his shoulder and saw Simon following. One of the workers pulled down a zip and held up a heavy plastic flap so they could enter.

The tent was divided up inside and several large showerheads dropped down from one of the metal pipes that ran along the length of the tent roof apex. A generator hummed away driving air through wide corrugated plastic tubes like some sort of mutated air conditioning system. 'We need your clothes, all of them,' one of the individuals shouted through the glass of the visor. A woman's voice. She stood back and held her gloved hands out. Ben just stood and looked at her, suddenly embarrassed at the thought that he was expected to strip in front of all of these people.

'It's all right Ben. We need to go through decontamination. They'll incinerate the clothes.'

Ben looked at his uncle who was already peeling off his clothing with the assistance of one of the workers. He stared at the livid black and purple bruises that had started to appear on his uncle's body from the fight with Tanaka. Was it really all over? Turning his back to the woman he slowly pulled down his pants and stepped out of them. Simon limped naked down the middle of the tent, a series of raised wooden slatted pallets formed a walkway over a metal collecting trough. Ben followed him and stopped under one of the showerheads.

'We need to use those and make sure we wash all over.' Simon pointed to a series of plastic containers and brushes. 'Just do what I do and follow along. Make sure you get under your nails too. This first one's going to be pretty hot and it'll stink from some sort of disinfectant they put in it. Shut your eyes and mouth. Just stand there and let it wash over you. The second shower will be a bit cooler and just water.' Ben heard someone shout 'Showers on', then gasped and swore as a spray of high-pressured hot water dropped down on him from above.

Chapter 29

It had been several hours before they were allowed to return to Simon's London apartment dressed in identical grey tracksuits and white trainers. After the showers they had to give blood, urine and saliva samples and were then transported to official looking buildings on the north side of the river. Ben and Simon were separated and interviewed by men in suits and military uniforms. Ben had to repeat his experiences over and over again to different people who seemed to be checking and cross checking his story. Eventually, after what seemed like hours of grilling, he was escorted to a room where Simon sat waiting for him.

While Simon prepared something for dinner, Ben had wanted another shower to get rid of the chemical smell on his skin left by the decontamination showers. They ate their pasta and a ready-made sauce in silence, Ben staring down at his plate as he forked the food round. After dinner Simon needed to check his computer so Ben turned on the television and waited for his uncle to return from his study.

'Here you go.' Simon handed Ben a steaming cup of tea. His nephew was wrapped in one of his own dressing gowns and tucked into the corner of the settee, legs drawn up under him. Ben took the tea from his uncle and turned back to the television. He stared at the news programme as images of the cordoned off VM Laboratories building were flashing across the screen. The journalist reported on the tragic accident that had resulted in the deaths of several people including the brilliant scientist and philanthropist Dr. Henrik von Moltke and claimed that the investigation into the accident would be thorough and long.

The VM laboratories article was then followed by an item on the sudden and shock resignation of Sir Nicholas Wellenby who, hours earlier, had resigned from the Cabinet and his position as Deputy Minister for Defence. He had decided to take early retirement to spend time with his family.

Ben watched in disbelief, the bubbling kernel of anger that had centred at the core of his being since he watched von Moltke succumb to his own infection erupted. 'What the hell is this?' he flung his hand out at the television set, eyes wide and fixed on Simon. 'They're not reporting the truth. That's nothing like what happened in there. What about Richard? What about the evil things von Moltke is guilty of doing? And there's nothing about the complicity of Gleeson and Wellenby? What was all that interviewing for? Getting me to tell them everything I knew? For what?'

Simon listened to his nephew's rant without reacting. He knew it was coming; in fact he would have been concerned if it hadn't. When Ben broke from his tirade Simon opened his mouth to speak, but Ben hadn't finished. 'You have something to do with this.' Ben jabbed his finger at Simon. 'You know why they're not reporting it properly. Did you know about my parents all along? This has something to do with your work. Admit it! I want to know. You owe it to me after everything I've done for you.'

Ben slumped back into the settee pulling the dressing gown around him like a shield against anything his uncle might tell him. Simon sat in silence for what seemed like ages, but was nothing more than a few seconds. He reached across for the television remote and pushed the standby button.

He rubbed his hands across his cheeks as he took a deep breath, the stubble making a rasping sound. As he exhaled he looked at Ben, 'Okay. You deserve to know, but I'm going to tell you a lot of stuff that has to remain secret, stuff I shouldn't be telling you. You listen to it, then you forget it. You understand?'

Ben didn't take his eyes off his uncle. He nodded once and waited for Simon to begin.

'I work for an organization known as MI9, the British Directorate of Military Intelligence, Section 9. During World War two it was a department of the War Office concerned with helping resistance movements in occupied Europe, in particular keeping escape routes open and providing professional assistance. After the war it was no longer needed and disbanded. Everyone has heard of MI5 and MI6, they're the departments the government uses to ensure security and surveillance, spy departments if you like. I started off working for MI6, but about ten years or so ago it was decided that the way the world was going they needed another department. One that, if necessary, operates outside both national and international law, one that very few people know about. That was when MI9 was secretly, and quietly, resurrected, but this time instead of working with resistance movements the department is all about eliminating threats, infiltrating and breaking down organisations, removing individuals that pose a danger to national and international security. Within the law and without violence if possible, but if not...' Simon left the sentence hanging.

'You mean assassinating people? Criminals? That was why you let von Moltke go ahead and release the spores? You knew he would die from it.'

Simon considered what Ben had said before nodding. 'There are some individuals who can't be reasoned with but they have the power, the arms, the technology and the money to cause a lot of harm, to kill a lot of innocent people. MI9 receives its information from both MI5 and MI6; we take over where they can't go. Because we often have to work outside the law we usually work alone too, no support from anywhere. If an agent goes down then they simply disappear, as if they never existed.'

'That's why mum and dad never knew much about what you did, or your life in general. Why you always came down to us in Leatherhead and we never came to see you.' Ben looked around the spacious apartment, 'Why I've never been here before now. You must have told a lot of lies to a lot of people.'

Simon nodded his head and for the first time he had to look away. His head dropped down and he picked at an imaginary thread on his tracksuit trousers. 'That's one part of the job that isn't easy. I try to avoid rather than lie if possible, but sometimes…yes, I lie a lot. It can't be any other way.'

Ben sat quiet waiting for more. He knew his silence was making his uncle feel uncomfortable, but he didn't care. 'What about the news reports?' he asked eventually.

'That's where the other departments come in; to cover things up. Von Moltke will no doubt be hailed a hero and a great loss to humanity in the coming days. The deaths of anyone else will be included in the tragic accident, which will no doubt be blamed on some sort of chemical leak or something like that. There will be no mention of what von Moltke was really working on or what he was trying to do. The children you found will be looked after and transferred to refugee centres, probably eventually sent out to foster homes. Their story will be recorded but dismissed as confused fantasy, bearing in mind everything they have been subjected to in their native countries. In a very short while this will all be history with a simple, but tragic explanation.'

'Try telling that to Mr. and Mrs. Osborne!'

'I'm sorry about Richard, truly I am, and if I could change things I would, but the real circumstances of his death can't be known. You understand that don't you?'

'Is that a threat? You have to silence me too if I say anything?'

'Ben please!' Simon sat forward, wincing at the pain from his bruised ribs. His eyes were pleading this time, no longer neutral. 'I'm trying to explain to you. I've told you far too much already, but I want you to understand.'

This time it was Ben's turn to look away, 'I know. I'm sorry,' he said quietly. He swallowed hard, 'And my parents?'

'It wasn't until I was in Alassio that I found out for sure that von Moltke and Gleeson were working together and that either one, or both, had been responsible for the bomb. It was probably Casoni and his henchmen who planted it. I was trying to gather more information when they captured me. I'd been watching their comings and goings on Gallinara and decided to take a closer look. It was clear they were moving something on and off the island. Those boxes were full of the compressed air rockets they planned to use for the spore release. Once they'd got the information they needed from your father's research they couldn't risk him still being around.'

Ben wiped away the tear that trickled down his cheek as he thought about his parents, so much had changed since their deaths; he had changed. He might be just sixteen, but any vestige of the child in him had disappeared when they perished and he embarked on his journey. He was no longer an innocent.

'I really thought they'd shot you back on Gallinara. I thought I'd lost you just like mum and dad.'

Simon looked puzzled for a second, 'Oh, that. A dart gun. They hit me with a fast acting tranquiliser that literally knocked me out straight away.'

They sat in silence for a few minutes. The low glass coffee table between them might well have been a yawning chasm. Ben lost in his own grief and confusion, Simon not knowing how to reach out to his nephew. It was Ben who eventually broke the impasse. 'I'm not going back to school,' he said his voice barely above a whisper.

'What? You don't have to think about things like that now.'

'I'm not going back to school.' Ben repeated more firmly. 'I've been thinking about it. I want to do what you do. There must be some sort of training, recruitment, whatever.'

'Now hang on a minute Ben. Your parents would want you to go and finish your education, university and then get a good job. Lead a normal life. You really don't want to live like me.'

'You seem to like it. It works for you and you do something good in the world. You earn good money, you travel, you do a service for your country; Queen and country, all that sort of thing. Surely you do a job that you should be proud of, so how can you tell me otherwise.'

Simon looked stunned, Ben's rationale was faultless and he couldn't think of an answer right there and then.

'You're too young Ben and your parents would never forgive me for letting you get into this.'

'My parents are dead.' The frankness of Ben's words hit Simon with the full force of their weight.

'Let's talk about it tomorrow. We're both tired and need to sleep.'

'I won't change my mind. I'm not going back to school.'

It was two days later when Simon announced that he needed to take Ben back to Luxborough House. Both of them had dodged around the subjects of MI9 and Ben's return to school, but when they had tentatively skirted around the subjects Ben remained steadfast in his decision.

During the two days Simon had spent a lot of the time in his study talking on the telephone, before he emerged and told Ben he needed to return to Leatherhead. Ben's heart sank at the thought of Aunt Evelyn and what she might have done to the place while he'd been away. As much as he now looked at his uncle as a person he never really knew, he preferred Simon's company to Evelyn's.

Ben remained quiet as Simon drove out of London heading down the A3. He stared ahead not really taking in the busy road or the sounds of some concerto on Classic FM that emanated from the speakers. He'd worked out it was two weeks before he was due to go back to school, so he had two weeks to make his guardians realise that he was serious about what he had said. He knew there would be hard battles ahead, but he equally knew he would not give in; his mind was made up.

As they headed to the Knoll roundabout Simon turned the radio off, 'Oh I forgot to tell you Evelyn and Harry won't be at Luxborough House, they've moved out. Gone back from whence they came.'

'What?' Ben sat up straight in his seat and stared at Simon, his mouth wide open. He hardly dared believe he'd heard his uncle correctly.

'Yes, seems they have had a rethink about things.' Simon looked at Ben and smiled.

'So who'll be there? I can't live there on my own?'

Simon laughed, 'It was just a few days ago you were telling me you were no longer a child and wanted to join MI9 and now you're telling me you can't take care of yourself!'

'But…' The car turned off the road and passed over the small single-track bridge. As the light shone through the trees and flickered on the windscreen Ben looked to his right and watched his family home as it came into view. Other than the front lawn being overgrown it didn't look that different from the outside. Ben feared for what the inside would look like though.

Simon hadn't stopped grinning since he had announced Evelyn and her husband wouldn't be there, like he was party to some private joke. Something was going on and Ben wasn't sure if he liked it or not. The gravel crunched under the tyres as Simon pulled to a stop. Ben got out of the car and stood looking at the heavy door framed by the gothic portico. He turned back to Simon who was leaning, arms crossed on the roof of the car, grinning stupidly. 'So what's the big joke?' When he heard the front door open he spun round; there, framed by the doorway, was the familiar figure of Mrs. Jessop.

'Oh Ben,' she said, her voice quivering as she rushed out and threw her arms around him gripping him tight.

'You're back,' said Ben stating the obvious when he could breathe again.

'Oh yes and back for good I hope.'

'Shall we tell him the rest of it?' Simon had come round the side of the car and was stood next to the pair.

'I reckon so,' said Mrs. J clasping her hands together and beaming.

Simon reached into his inner jacket pocket and pulled out a slim white envelope. He opened it and removed a single sheet of stiff, expensive looking paper. He unfolded it slowly and passed it over to Ben.

Ben read in silence, aware that the air around him was electric with expectation from his uncle and Mrs. J. He read one part over and over again before he looked up at the expectant pair.

'*...that Simon Michael Weir and Molly Josephine Jessop are appointed the legal guardians of Benjamin Henry Weir...*'

'You mean…'

'Yes,' said Simon. 'Evelyn's agreed to give up her guardianship in favour of Mrs. J. We'll both be moving in here and making sure you don't get up to any mischief.'

Ben hesitated for a brief second as the news sank in and then, throwing the letter in the air, let out a huge cry of relief and launched himself at his uncle and Mrs. J, pulling them into a group hug.

About the Author

Neil writes in a range of different genres and under several pseudonyms. This is the first fiction book under his own name and he hopes to be able to bring you the second episode in Ben's adventures before too long.

A former scientist and lecturer Neil is based in the UK.

You can follow Neil on Twitter @NeilSlade3 where you will find announcements as to how the second book is coming along and its release date etc.

www.neilsladeauthor.com
FB: Neil Slade Author
Tw: @NeilSlade3
Insta: @Odinsbones